ELEANOR MERRY

Dead Aware 2

No Place Like Home

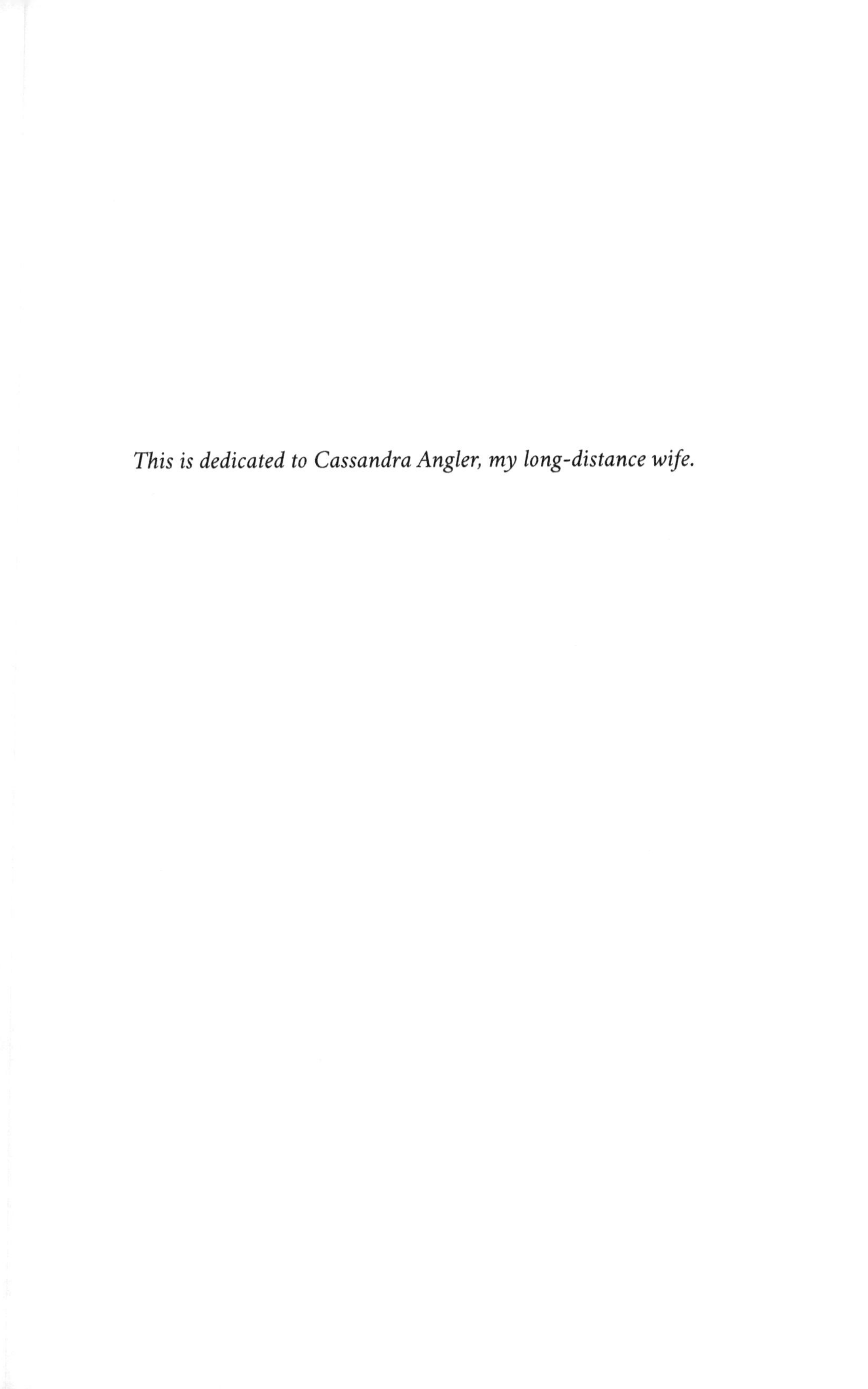

This is dedicated to Cassandra Angler, my long-distance wife.

Contents

Preface iii

Dead Aware 2: No Place Like Home By Eleanor Merry iv

Prologue 1

Chapter 1 3

Chapter 2 7

Chapter 3 14

Chapter 4 19

Chapter 5 23

Chapter 6 29

Chapter 7 33

Chapter 8 39

Chapter 9 46

Chapter 10 54

Chapter 11 60

Chapter 12 67

Chapter 13 78

Chapter 14 87

Chapter 15 92

Chapter 16 100

Chapter 17 105

Chapter 18 112

Chapter 19 114

Chapter 20 121

Chapter 21 126

Chapter 22 130

Chapter 23 138

Chapter 24 140

Chapter 25	141
Chapter 26	148
Chapter 27	152
Chapter 28	157
Chapter 29	160
Chapter 30	167
Chapter 31	176
Chapter 32	181
Chapter 33	187
Chapter 34	195
Chapter 35	198
Chapter 36	202
Chapter 37	205
Prologue	208

Preface

MY FIGHT
Scott Deegan
It wasn't my fight
I was just a kid
Spending my days
Doing what kids did
It wasn't my fight
I didn't understand your hate
Us and them
A need to segregate
It wasn't my fight
I approached in trust
Offered friendship
You crushed it into dust
It wasn't my fight
Until the real you appeared
Taught me your kind
Was something to be feared
It wasn't my fight
That was before
You pushed too far
Time to settle the score
This is now my fight
You will know my strength
When you know my story
You'll never be the same.

Dead Aware 2: No Place Like Home By Eleanor Merry

It's been seven years since the FIRE virus devastated the globe, leaving most of the world population decimated. From the wreckage, infected and non-infected survivors emerge to find their new places in the world.

Since rising after the infection, Max and Clara abscond to the British Columbia wilderness to live in peace away from the rest of the world. Their life is hard but happy until outside forces tear their family apart in efforts to find a cure for FIRE. Max and Clara must leave their home and once more go against the people who consider them no more than 'zombies'. With the help of new and old friends, will they be able to finally overcome humanity's prejudice against them?

Dead Aware: No Place Like Home is book 2 in the Dead Aware series and is best enjoyed after reading Dead Aware: A Zombie Journey
You can sign up for my newsletter to receive a free Dead Aware story, Zombie Mom

Prologue

In the darkness they crouched, hiding from the people pursuing them. Dots of light could be seen coming closer in the distance and Clara stifled a moan as she held her belly. Though the cold didn't affect them, their breath was visible in the moonlight of the deep winter night. Helping his wife up, Max hurried them through the forest in the other direction, determined to keep Clara away from the grasp of the uninfected after them.

Clara escaped from a military compound that had been experimenting on people like them, who had been infected by the FIRE virus, several months ago. Ever since, she and Max avoided people as much as possible. When she escaped, she was in the very early stages of pregnancy; since then, however, her belly had grown, and it was now plain to see she was pregnant. The day before, they had been spotted by a group of uninfected who immediately noticed the pregnant 'zombie' and ever since, she and Max had been running.

"Come on baby, just a bit further," Max whispered to her as they tore through the dense pines. "I've got you, Clara. I won't let you go…."

* * *

One Month Later

"I can't do it!" Clara cried, sweat and tears running down her face.

"You can do this, Clara," Max encouraged, wiping her face with a damp cloth as he watched with worry and love in his eyes. "You've got this, baby. I'm here."

"Aargggh!!" Clara screamed as another contraction ran through her body, making her feel as though she was being ripped in two. An overwhelming urge to push came over her, but she was so tired and weak.

"I can see something!" Max exclaimed. "Push, baby! You're almost there!"

With the end in sight, Clara cried out as she pushed with everything she had. And again. And again. Finally, on her fourth push she felt something within her give and was filled with both a profound feeling of loss and gain as a small cry filled the air. Dropping her head, she watched Max grab a small deerskin blanket she had made and wrap a tiny bundle up in it. Tears filled his eyes as he brought the tiny creature up to her. Despite her shaking limbs, Clara reached out to bring the small bundle to her chest and looked down onto the face of her child for the first time.

"It's a girl," Max whispered as he handed their daughter to her, wonder in his voice. "You did it, baby."

* * *

Three Months Later

"What do you think?" Clara asked as she hugged their infant daughter, Joan, tighter to her body. The wind on the coast was unforgiving and cold this time of year, but the prospect of a safe place for them was too good to pass up. They had been traveling the British Columbia coast for weeks and, with the fall approaching, knew they needed to find a place soon.

She looked up to Max, who was looking at the island in the distance. Though they couldn't see around the outcropping of rocks jutting from the water between them and it, the island appeared to be a decent size, and they couldn't see anyone from their vantage point.

"It could work," Max finally replied cryptically. "Maybe I should go alone to check it out first?" Clara frowned at him as the baby began to cry, bouncing in place as she replied, "Then I'll just be alone here with the baby anyways. That isn't any safer. We all go."

Max seemed to consider this for a moment before nodding.

"Okay, go into the tree cover out of the wind while I grab that boat we saw."

Chapter 1

Six Years Later

Joan stared down into the puddle, admiring the pale glow of her skin in the early morning light. The ripples on the surface made it difficult to distinguish her features, but the fair skin and eyes are not to be mistaken. The mark of the infected. Not that Joan truly understood what that meant. She had never seen someone who didn't look like her and, in fact, never met anyone apart from her parents.

She had never seen a mirror before either, so whenever she had an opportunity to see her reflection, she was fascinated. She knew her parents had similar features, similar colouring, but the chance to see herself up close was always something she relished. She once asked what they looked like before the infection, but all her father told her was that her mother was now more beautiful than ever. Unlike both of her parents, she was born looking this way. Joan had never experienced the brain damage caused by the FIRE virus and, consequently, her mother teased that she was the smartest (and cutest) zombie around. Usually when she said this, her father would tighten his mouth and tell her not to call them zombies. Joan also didn't really know what that meant, but knew it was a word for people that looked like them.

Joan would ask her parents about their life before the virus, for clues and details of what the outside world was like, but usually her dad would close up and not say anything. Her mom would occasionally give her small glimpses, little memories and tidbits. Never anything important though. Nothing truly interesting to her six-year-old mind. Despite her interest and longing for the outside world, Joan loved her parents. She loved the ocean and the forest, to explore and see new things. None of them could ever have anticipated that this curiosity and desire to explore would trigger the events that would change all their lives forever.

* * *

"Jo baby, come inside! It's time for breakfast!" Clara yelled, her voice carrying through the trees. She knew Joan liked to spend her mornings wandering and being on her own and Clara often wondered how such an outgoing child could also enjoy her solitude as much as she did. *Not that she has much choice,* Clara thought wryly.

It didn't take long for a small white figure to come dashing through the trees, throwing her arms around Clara's middle. Smiling down at her, Clara ushered her daughter inside for breakfast.

As Joan took her seat, Clara placed the eggs and fish on the uneven table. Like most of their furniture, Max had crafted it for them years ago. Whenever Clara thought back to some of his earlier attempts, she equally cringed and tried not to laugh. Being on their own had been quite a learning curve, but one that Max and her had taken to with gusto.

The spring after they found their island haven, Max had adventured to the mainland to find things for their home. He came back a week later with supplies in tow having found an abandoned summer camp a few days away. Not only was he able to get more clothes and blankets, but he also found several pots and buckets, a few knives, and even a small case of matches. He had ventured out a few times over the years, but most of their belongings were gifts of the forest and sea.

They arrived at their current home, an island off the coast of Northern British Columbia, almost five years before. It was a few kilometers wide and long, big enough to not feel enclosed or trapped, small enough to keep well protected.

When Clara was pregnant, she and Max travelled far and went through various temporary homes with ranges of success. It had been a stressful time in their lives, but Max had been determined to find the perfect spot to keep his family safe. Joan's birth was about as smooth as it could be, but had left Clara incredibly weak, making travel all the more difficult.

They finally came upon the island when Joan was only a few months old. Far enough away from the mainland, and big enough to look tempting, they had taken a boat they found along the shore and rowed out. In the centre of the island they even found a small cabin, not much more than a large shed, that had some very old fishing gear inside. Max had since made significant improvements and now they boasted a four-room home that was warm and dry, even in the winter. In the summer, like now, it was a beautiful haven and Clara usually left the door open to let the light shine through into their modest home.

"How was your morning, sweetie?" Clara asked as Joan pounced on her breakfast, causing Clara to smile. She loved that her daughter had such a healthy appetite.

"It was good, mama," Joan replied with her mouth full. "The rain made everything real pretty and I found a cool spider web that was really shiny! It had so many drops!"

"That sounds beautiful." Clara imagined the spiral web with small silver droplets. She loved listening to the things Joan described finding in the forest. Parental pride filled both her and Max often at their young girl's incredible insights and view of the world.

Clara was watching her daughter scoop food into her mouth when a pang of sadness struck her. Although there were still gaps in her memory, she knew enough about how the world once was to know Joan didn't have a typical childhood. She never got to play with friends, have birthday parties or toys. She would never go to school with kids her age or experience so many things children should.

Max and Clara did their best with what they had. Clara taught Joan letters, numbers, and other things at a young age, as much as she could with their limited resources. Max crafted small toys for his daughter; wooden figures and other things. Joan didn't know what she was missing and, consequently, was very mature for her young age in many ways while being incredibly naïve in others. While Clara knew that where they were now was the best place for them, she sometimes regretted their decision to live in solitude. At least if they were with other people, Joan may have someone to play with.

Sighing, Clara shifted her attention back to her meal.

Chapter 2

Max had learned a lot about living in the forest over the years, including how to weave through the thick trees and brush, even in the middle of a dry summer, without making a sound. With infinite patience and caution, he made his way toward his quarry. His patience paid off, and the doe before him remained calm and unafraid as he approached unseen.

Sweat dripped down his face, but his infected body didn't register the heat. Wiping the salty drops from his eyes, he wound up and flung the heavy stone in his sling with perfect accuracy, downing and stunning the deer. He ran up behind it and used his club to finish the job, his chest heaving with exhilaration. With no time to revel in his catch, he swiftly pulled out his knife to bleed the animal and prepare it to bring home.

Max had grown incredibly strong through his daily routine. He had vague memories of his own childhood, and hunting with whom he assumed was his own father. Re-teaching himself the skills needed to survive hadn't been any real hardship. In fact, he enjoyed the challenge of it and the sense of accomplishment he felt providing for his family.

As he went through the familiar motions, he thought of the rest of the things he needed to do today.

Check and reset fish traps. Get the girls to help section the deer meat. Fix that leak in the bedroom ceiling while the weather stays nice.

In reality, he loved the busy schedule and how it kept his mind occupied. He had noticed long ago that during those slower moments, in particular in the winter, his mind would wander outward, and he would think about what was going on in the rest of the world. Every so often they would see other people, infected and otherwise, on the far shores. Their home was set back far enough from the shoreline and was blocked in places by natural rock formations, so others couldn't see them unless they came across. The only boat for miles was their own, which Max used to make trips back and forth to gather supplies and hunt. In truth, a good swimmer could probably make the journey from the mainland, but the appearance of their small island didn't boast anything worth the effort. Staying hidden and keeping to themselves had ensured their survival these past years, and Max did everything he could to keep their home private.

As he finished removing the deer's organs, he placed a few key pieces aside and began to work on the heavy skin. While they didn't keep all the skins of the animals they hunted, deerskin was particularly good as once it was treated it tended to be water resistant, yet breathable and durable. Max smiled to himself when he thought of the first one he had brought home so many years ago. Clara made a small blanket for their newborn daughter, which she still used to this day.

Once the skin was removed, the last thing for Max to do was separate and remove the legs to make the pieces easier to carry. His muscles flexed with effort as he began to make the trips to and from the boat. It was only mid-morning, and already he had secured enough meat to feed his family for a month or more. Although it was early in the season, they would likely dry the deer meat, eating the fish and seafood that was so abundant.

Taking the time to ensure his tracks weren't obvious on the shoreline, Max made his way back across the water.

* * *

"Mom! Mom! I think daddy caught something big!" Joan exclaimed as she ran up the clearing. Her father rarely let her off the island, and she had a habit of watching from the tree's when he would come home. She had been taught to remain unseen, something Max had taught her from a young age.

"Good, baby. Why don't you run down and give him a hand then? I just need to finish the washing here and I'll come join you." Clara smiled at her daughter, who barely waited for the sentence to leave her mother's mouth before bounding down to the water. Humming to herself, Clara dipped her hands back into the large bucket she used for laundry.

She had discovered long ago that yucca or clematis, two native plants, acted as a sort of natural soap. Clara would use that or various citrus fruits to clean everything from clothes to dishes. On one of Max's first forays into the outside world, he had grabbed a few books. It had taken them both some time, but they both managed to remember how to read, despite the brain damage brought on by the virus. While neither did so for leisure, Max had found a few textbooks, including one about flora and fauna in British Columbia. It had been an invaluable asset to learn more about their homeland and how to survive.

Clara's first attempts at soap hadn't worked as well as she had hoped. The book had listed multiple options of plants that would create saponins, which foamed up and created a soap-like substance. The first plant she had tried, being the most easily accessible to her, had been horse chestnuts. What she didn't know, however, was that if you don't skin them, the peels can dye your skin. A few days, and two brown-dyed hands later, she moved on to alternatives.

Despite her failure, the memory was a fond one. Max had found her, dyed to her elbows with a dismayed look on her face, and laughed. His laughter had quickly turned her dismay into anger. Seeing this, he swiftly scooped her up, despite her being heavily pregnant at the time, and took her to their bed. She could still remember how her dyed hands looked against his skin. Clara smiled when she thought of how that day ended and wondered if she and Max could sneak away later.

As she hung up the last of the laundry, she heard a faint but deep laugh followed by a high-pitched squeal from down by the shore. She smiled and wiped her hands, before heading down to greet her family.

* * *

For most of the afternoon, the three of them worked to prepare the venison.

They kept aside some fresh meat for the coming days, but much of it would be processed to keep through the winter. They had a variety of methods to do this, all modified to keep their modest home safe.

Looking over at his wife and daughter, who were both sweating freely at the exertion of the task before them, Max felt a surge of pride. When he had made the decision to leave with Clara so many years before, he hadn't really known how they would be able to survive. Keeping her safe and away from people had been his biggest priority, in particular because she was pregnant at the time.

Before they left their home for the last time, Max had spoken at length with Rachel, a doctor who studied virology. Rachel had helped Clara and a group of other infected escape from a particularly cruel military compound after discovering she was pregnant. While Max hadn't known Clara was pregnant at the time, Rachel had told him much about the virus and what he could expect for themselves in the coming months and years. She had guessed that over the next six to eight months (a time concept he hadn't quite grasped at the time) people like him and Clara, infected who remained relatively stable, would regain much of their former abilities and memories. Luckily, Rachel had been right. While there were still bits of their past that were forever lost, they were much the same people as they were before the virus with only a few key differences.

The sun was lowering in the sky when they finally finished. Clara had started cooking a deer roast in her ingenious ground oven earlier in the day, and Max's stomach rumbled at the thought. Joan laughed at her father, who swiftly tossed her over his shoulder and carried her up to the house for dinner. She giggled the whole way.

* * *

Max woke with the sun. With life in the wilderness, and with them needing to be careful of attracting attention with lights or fire, the sun going down typically meant they did as well. Consequently, Max had gotten used to taking advantage of every moment of light.

Careful not to disturb Clara or Joan, who were currently wrapped up together in their family-sized bed, he crept out of the room with his clothes in hand.

After dressing he grabbed his tool belt, a modified fanny pack, and made his way out of the house. First on his list was to check the fishing traps. Smiling, he stretched his arms to the sun, grateful for the warm summer weather. Before he made it more than a few feet from the house, he heard the gentle creak of the door behind him.

"You should be back in bed with your mother," he teased, turning to smile at his daughter. He was rewarded with a brilliant grin and two small arms around his waist.

"But I want to go with you, daddy," Joan pleaded. Max stared into her eyes for a moment before smiling.

"Go tell your mother so she doesn't worry."

With another giant smile she ran back into the house.

One of the consequences of what he and Clara had been through was a personal flaw Max admitted to readily: he was overprotective of his wife and daughter. He had spent weeks separated from Clara and in that time the feeling of helplessness almost consumed him. Max never wanted to experience that feeling of not knowing again and did everything he could to keep both his girls safe and close to home.

For the most part they both tolerated his anxiety well. Clara in particular understood the perils of the world, and while she still felt stifled by him at times, she understood where Max was coming from. Joan, however, was a different matter. The young girl wanted to know everything about everything. She had a curious and adventurous spirit that spilled out into everything she did. Max had tried taking her out with him before, but typically ended up getting less done as a result. Today, however, with the sun shining, he thought some quality time with his daughter was exactly what he needed.

"So the line goes here, and you put it back in place like this," Max patiently showed Joan how to reset the fish traps. "Later on, we can come back and see if there are any more."

The small girl vibrated with excitement, obviously thrilled at being included in her father's rituals.

"Can I help you hunt next time too?" she begged. Max furrowed his brow slightly as he considered her request.

The fish traps were an invaluable part of their everyday life. While Max did try to go hunting when he could, seafood was a dietary staple for them in particular because it contained so much of the protein they all craved. Hunting deer or other animals meant leaving their island, which was always a risk and not one he wanted to expose either Clara or Joan to. Clara didn't really mind and was kept occupied by her own daily chores and managing their home. Her nesting instinct had kicked in fiercely after Joan was born. Max's heart squeezed at the thought of how she had turned their little house into a home.

Looking down at Joan's sweet face, despite knowing how she was manipulating him with that smile, Max softened. He knew he couldn't keep her here forever, so teaching her more about the outside world was inevitable and necessary.

"Okay, baby." Joan squealed and danced around him. "Next time I go hunting you can come too." She wrapped her arms around her father's waist once more and squeezed tightly.

"Thanks, daddy. I love you."

"I love you too, baby."

* * *

It was only a few weeks later when Max declared that the next morning they would be going hunting. Variety was always well received, and they had gone through the fresh deer meat long before, saving the dried strips they had treated for their winter stockpile. Fortunately, they didn't typically get too much snow, not being too far north, and were able to fish most of the year. Even still, storing supplies in the warmer months was a necessity.

Joan bounced off the walls all evening, excited to join her father in what she expected to be an epic adventure. While she was kept busy most of the time, her youthful spirit craved more.

"What are you thinking?" Clara asked Max as she cleared the table after their dinner.

"Well," Max replied, "that deer was a bit of a fluke. Usually they're mostly around in the spring. We can try for beaver or even a couple of rabbits. We'll try to be back by nightfall, but I'll bring our sleeping bags just in case."

Before Clara could respond Joan shrieked excitedly. "You mean we can have a SLEEPOVER, daddy?"

Max chuckled softly, looking over to his wife's smiling face. "We'll see, sweetie."

Chapter 3

Joan jumped up the moment she felt Max move the following morning. Clara groaned and rolled over, allowing their daughter to hop from the bed. Max chuckled quietly to himself as he watched Clara; She had never been a morning person. Joan, however, was more like Max in this way and preferred to rise early.

"Is it time to go, daddy?" she whispered excitedly as she exited their bedroom. Staying quiet to let Clara sleep, they had a quick breakfast and set off.

The sky was slightly grey, betraying the humidity that Max knew would soon be coming. They each had backpacks with some supplies, including layers of clothing and some dried fish. Max hoped to be able to eat fresh tonight, but knew not to rely on it. While mother nature was bountiful, you couldn't be too careful.

The two made their way down to the shore where their boat was hidden. Max had made a hiding place in a small crevasse in the rocks so it wouldn't be visible from the opposite side, but was easy to access when they needed. Max showed Joan how the boat was tied up and how to get in without getting wet, then how to push off from the beach. They hadn't gone to the mainland together since the year prior, and Joan had grown up considerably since. While she was only six, she was a smart girl and caught on fast to what Max was showing her. He didn't recall having much interaction with young children before FIRE but felt sure that Joan was advanced for her age in many ways. Without further delay, they rowed the gap to the far bank. He showed her the best way to row with the least effort and how to find the current that would take them toward the shore.

Truthfully, Max loved the journey across the water. The fresh ocean air, the vastness surrounding him. Even the exertion of rowing was welcome. Looking over at Joan he could see her eyes were closed, taking it all in. He smiled at himself. *She surely is my daughter.*

Max led them over to a small inlet he favoured for these trips. Dense trees surrounded it, making it a good spot to disembark without attracting attention, as well as providing many spots to hide the boat.

On one of his first forays across after finding the island, Max had destroyed every boat he could find in the vicinity. He worried at times what would happen if they ever lost theirs, but the desire to ensure the island stayed inaccessible was stronger. If need be, they could find other ways across.

Max waded into the waist-deep water to pull the boat the last few feet to the shore. Although he knew the water was cold, it didn't bother him. Before he could make the last of the gap, he heard a loud splash behind him. Gasping, he turned around in time to see Joan's head popping up out of the water, a mischievous smile on her face.

"I can help too!" She swam over to where Max was and grabbed a hold of another rope. He grinned back at her before showing her how to pull the boat ashore, tie it down, and hide it with thick leaves.

By the time they were finished, the warmth of the day, despite the grey skies, had mostly dried their clothes. Before they grabbed their bags, Max took Joan by the hands and sat her down on a moss-covered rock nearby.

"Listen, sweetie," Max began, trying to stay serious, "I am very happy to have you with me today. Your mother and I are both so proud of you and how much you have been learning and trying to help more." At this, Joan smiled, nodding eagerly. She loved her parents praise and always wanted them to be happy with her.

"Today we are going to go for a hike and see what we can find. I don't know if we will find anything to hunt, but if not I'll teach you a few more things instead. This is very important, though. You need to listen to *everything* I tell you, without hesitating. If I say hide, you hide. If I say run, you run. If I say dance like a chicken, you do it. Okay?" Joan giggled at the last one, causing Max to reach out his arms. She immediately threw herself into them, hugging her father close. "Okay, daddy."

By midmorning, they still hadn't seen much wildlife except for the occasional squirrel and the birds that sang around them. Max had shown Joan how to set a snare trap and was proud when she set the next one completely by herself. They had been following a small stream, wanting to stay close to what Max knew was a main source of water for nearby animals. They took a short break to nibble on some dried fish as well as a few berries they had collected along the way. While their kind did crave protein above all else, Clara and he had discovered long ago their bodies needed other types of nutrients to function to their fullest capacities.

As they sat by the gentle flowing water, Max studied his daughter, who was whistling. When she was quite young, she had been enamored by the birds and had spent countless days learning how to imitate them. Now, at six, she could literally whistle the birds out of the sky. Max wondered if he should be using this skill more for hunting, but didn't want to disturb the beautiful scene in front of him.

Joan sat in the middle of a clearing, perfectly still except her lips, which warbled along with a nearby chickadee. The small bird had swooped down and sat only a few feet in front of her, staring at her with a cocked head as she whistled back the simple two-note song. A moment later, two more small birds flew down even closer, answering her call. Joan's smile was magnificent as her bird friends chirped and hopped around her. A mischievous smile crossed her face, and she glanced over at Max, making him wonder what the girl was up to. A moment later, she let out a loud *caw*, effectively causing her small friends to flutter away.

Her laugh carried over the clearing, quickly joined by Max.

"That wasn't very nice, little bird," Max smirked at her. Joan blushed slightly, but didn't comment as she made her way back over to him.

"Daddy?" She asked sweetly. He narrowed his eyes at her. He had been a parent long enough to know a child's tricks, and his daughter certainly knew how to use her adorableness to her own advantage.

"Yes?" he asked sweetly back, playing along with her game.

"Can I go into the forest just a little ways? I won't go far and I'll be right back!" Joan exclaimed, foreseeing his objections. Max considered this and despite his initial feelings to keep her beside him, he was in a good mood and she had been listening well all morning. Their last trip had almost ended very badly, but she had grown up a lot since then. Max pretended to think about it for a moment longer, placing his hand to his chin.

"Hmmm, I don't know..." he teased.

"Puuleasee!"

He smiled, "Okay. But don't go far and stay where I can hear you. We will leave in ten minutes." He was rewarded with a kiss on his cheek before his daughter pranced off into the forest.

* * *

Joan continued skipping ahead, thrilled at the freedom of being out with her father. She loved their island and wandering through it, but the unexplored and illustrious mainland was an adventure she had been longing for. The last time her father brought her, she wandered off while he was distracted and ended up in a bear cave. Luckily, Max realized she was missing and managed to get her out before she disturbed the occupants. This time, she was determined not to get into any trouble so her father would take her out more.

She slowed her walk and looked around at the green surrounding her. Some plants she recognized from her own island; pines, spruces, and hemlocks all dotted the landscape. Her eyes widened as she saw a flash of red hiding behind a vibrant green vine. Walking over, she lifted the vine to uncover a large and untouched raspberry bush. Her favourite! Grabbing a large leaf to carry them, she began to pick her prizes. It only took a moment before her hands and arms started to itch.

She dropped the vine she had lifted, as well as the raspberries she had already picked, so she could scratch. After only a minute the itching got worse, and she began to panic as red dots began to rise on her skin. Her eyes widened, and she yelled, "Dadddy!!"

* * *

Max had been sitting enjoying the peaceful sounds of the forest when he heard Joan call for him. The alarm was evident in her voice and he ran as fast as he could. He found her in a small clearing, raspberries spilled around her feet. She was panicking, rubbing her hands and arms furiously, punctuated by small shrieks. Rushing over to her, he immediately noted the ivy covering the raspberry bush behind her. He knew his daughter's penchant for berries, and did his best not to smile at her plight, knowing it wouldn't help the situation.

Grabbing her face in his hands and doing his best to avoid the plant, he looked into her eyes.

"Joan! Are you okay, baby?" She sobbed as she looked at her father. "Daddy what is happening to me? It's so itchy!" Her pale limbs were covered in red dots, surrounded by angry pink skin from her scratching. There was no poison ivy on their island, but he recognized the plant well enough.

"You'll be okay, sweetie." Max used a stick and lifted one of the vibrant vines covering the raspberry bush. "This plant is called poison ivy. It makes you itchy and gives you rashes but it isn't dangerous, just uncomfortable. Come on, I have some stuff that will make it better." Leaving the liberated raspberries, he led her back to the stream where he instructed her to put her arms into the cool water.

"This will help a bit, and so will your mother's special salve. Let me get it; keep your hands in there for now." Joan nodded, her eyes still fearful but glad her father was here to help her.

Distracted as he was searching through his backpack, Max didn't notice the approaching footsteps until a voice called out behind them.

"Having trouble, friend?"

Chapter 4

Max froze at the sound of the unfamiliar voice before slowing turning. Behind them were three men, all with pale skin and eyes. Max relaxed slightly as he realized they were also infected, but still moved in front of his daughter protectively.

Joan stared at the men, her itchiness forgotten and her eyes wide. She had never seen anyone other than her mother or father so close before.

"We are fine, *friend*," Max responded cautiously. It had been quite a while since he had run into anyone in this area and he wondered where these men had come from.

While all three men had similar complexions, they were very different otherwise. The one who spoke was a huge dark-haired man with a scruffy beard covering his face. To his left was a blond man about Max's height who had long straggly hair. The third man had lighter hair as well, but his eyes seemed more vacant than the others. The expression on his face reminded Max of Jay.

"We heard screamin' and came to see what was happening," the dark-haired man commented. All three of them stared at Joan, causing Max to tighten his fists.

"Yes," Max replied tersely, "we had a run in with some ivy. We're fine though, and need to be on our way." He turned slightly to look down at Joan, who was still staring at the men with wide eyed fascination. Max shifted his foot slightly, indicating she should get up. Shaking her head slightly she stood, staying behind her father. The men continued to stare at Joan, and a slight growl picked up in Max's throat in warning.

Disregarding the sound, dark hair turned his attention back to Max momentarily.

"Quite young for one of us," he commented. "Most of the young didn't survive the initial outbreak." It wasn't until then Max realized the real reason for their interest in his daughter, and he sighed slightly. Joan peeked around his waist.

"True," Max replied, "but she wasn't born during the initial outbreak and never had the virus. She was born this way." Dark and blond's eyes both widened.

"Born like that?" Blond gasped. Max paused, regretting his own wisdom in disclosing that to the strange men. Looking down to his daughter, he nodded his head in the direction of their packs. She quickly scurried over and started packing up their last few belongings. Once he saw she was following his direction, Max turned his attention back to the men.

"Yes," he replied simply. "Now we should be on our way." Dark hair looked at him for a long moment and Max could almost see the wheels in his head turning. Finally, the man gave Max a smile that didn't quite reach his eyes.

"We understand," dark hair continued to smile as he extended his hand to Max. "I'm Bear. This is Squid and Steve." Bear nodded his head at Steve, "he don't talk none, but when I found him, Steve was wanderin' around in a blue uniform with his name tag." Steve perked up slightly at hearing his name, staring intently at Bear. Max stared down at the proffered hand for a moment before turning to grab one of the heavy bags from Joan.

"I'm Max. This is Joan. Nice to meet you gentlemen, but we still must be on our way."

"So, Max," Squid said, assuming an air of casualness, "you guys live around here?" Max paused at the question, but did his best to appear unaffected.

"Nope," Max replied, causing Joan to widen her eyes at the lie, "just passing through." Bear gave a knowing grin and nodded.

"Well, was nice meeting you folks anyways."

As Joan and Max walked away, the three men didn't take their eyes off them. Max hurried Joan forward without looking back.

For the next hour, Max led them on a winding route through the forest rather than directly back to the alcove where they had left the boat. He kept a firm grip on her arm for much of it until he looked down and noticed the handprint he had left on her delicate skin. He released his hold and paused to kiss her forehead before continuing.

* * *

"Daddy," Joan finally whispered, "who were those people?"

For several minutes, Max didn't respond. He was chiding himself for taking her out at all, much less admitting to the strangers that she had been born with the look of an infected. Their interest concerned him greatly, and he was loath to tell Clara when they got home.

"Just men, baby," he finally replied, trying to keep his voice calm. "You saw how their skin was like ours?" Joan nodded. "That means they were infected with FIRE, like mommy and daddy."

Joan seemed to think about this for a moment. "That means they got sick, right?" Max nodded and Joan looked down at the pale skin on her arm, mottled as it was with red spots.

"Does that mean I got sick too, daddy?" Again, Max paused before answering.

"No," he finally replied. Joan didn't ask any more questions despite her burning curiosity. If everyone else who looked like them had gotten sick, why hadn't she?

The rest of the afternoon was a bit of a blur as Max led Joan through the strange route to get back to the boat. She had asked about the snare traps they had set, but Max told her they would have to leave them. Joan didn't quite comprehend the danger of their sanctuary being found and was beginning to get angry.

"But I set them myself! I wanna see if I caught something!" she argued indignantly.

"Joan," Max sighed and rubbed his face, "it isn't important, okay? I have other things to worry about right now like getting you home safe."

"But why? Those guys seemed nice. I wanna check the traps!" Joan continued arguing. Already emotional about the situation, Max snapped back, "Stop! You don't know what you are talking about. Hurry up, we have to go." He moved forward, only pausing when he realized she was still standing behind him, arms crossed not moving in the middle of the trail.

"Come on!"

"No!"

Max felt his face redden. They didn't have time for this. He stomped back over to her, doing his best to keep a rein on his anger.

"Joan," he said through a strained voice, "we need to go. Now. It isn't safe. You don't know what people are like. Please. Come."

Max watched his daughter's face go through a range of emotions, settling on anger.

"Well, I would know more if you and mom told me *anything!*" she shouted at him. "You guys treat me like a baby and it's not fair!"

"You are a baby!" Max shouted back, unable to keep his temper in check any longer. "NOW, Joan." He continued back on the trail, not waiting this time to see if she would follow.

Joan stood there a moment, still furious with her father. When she realized he wasn't going to wait for her, she ran to catch up.

I'll show you who's a baby, she thought.

Chapter 5

Max and Joan were silent the rest of the way home. They were coming back empty handed, except for a rash and two foul moods. It was late in the afternoon by the time they returned. As soon as they walked up the clearing to their home, Clara could sense something had gone wrong.

"Hey guys, how was your day?" Clara asked them, hoping she was reading them wrong. Joan huffed and continued past without a word as Clara watched her in bewilderment. She looked to Max for clarification as their daughter disappeared into the tree's.

"What happened?"

Even though she knew there was a chance Max and Joan wouldn't be back that night, Clara had still prepared a full dinner in case they had. She put the final touches on everything while Max told her what had happened.

"How far away were they?" Clara asked worriedly.

"Not nearly far enough," Max replied. "I've been on this route a few times and never seen anyone before. Maybe some people have moved into the area. Or maybe they were passing through. We didn't stay long enough to ask." Clara nodded and considered the situation. She trusted Max and his judgement, and the fact that he was so worried about the infected men's interest in Joan made her heart clench in fear.

"What should we do?" she asked him, a slight waver in her voice. In hearing this, Max stepped over to her and enveloped her in a hug. "We do what we always do," Max whispered into her hair, "we stay careful and quiet. We stick to fishing on the far side of the island for a while. No more mainland visits for Joan, or me for a while. It'll be okay, sweetie."

Clara relaxed into Max's arms, grateful for the comfort. She knew he was right. They just needed to be a bit extra careful, that was all.

"Okay." She gave him a small smile and a kiss. "I'll go find Joan."

* * *

Joan had run to her favourite spot on the island, at the mouth of a small cave near the west side. A small clearing surrounded it with blackberry bushes growing in abundance. The cave was no more than twenty feet deep but was perfect for a little girl. She kept many of her "toys" and other things inside, and both of her parents respected this as her own little space.

Today, however, Joan wasn't enjoying her favourite place like she usually would. She sat sullenly on a small bench her father had crafted, kicking her feet at the ground. While mature for her age, she was still a child and still learning how to handle different emotions. Her frame of mind switched between angry then sad and then back to angry in a matter of minutes, leaving her feeling exhausted and depressed.

They never tell me anything. Stupid mom and dad. I'm not a little kid anymore and that's all they treat me like. Those other guys seemed totally nice they didn't seem so bad. They've never let me meet anyone. Shoulda let me check the traps....

On and on, these loops played in Joan's head. She was so distracted by her own outrage she almost didn't hear the crack of a twig outside the cave. Shooting her head up, Joan looked up into her mother's clear blue eyes. For a moment the young girl's resolve cracked as she saw the love in Clara's eyes, but her anger quickly won out.

* * *

Clara watched as the expressions crossed Joan's face. Confusion and anger as she approached, a softening when she looked into her eyes and then finally a fierce sort of determination. *Her father's daughter alright....*

Clara walked over to the small bench and sat beside her daughter before saying anything.

"Your father told me what happened. Do you wanna talk about it?" Clara asked gently.

"Did he tell you he's a big poopy meanie who never lets me do anything?" Joan huffed. Clara bit her lip to hold back a laugh at her young daughter's tantrum. She was a mother, and not unused to the outrage of a young girl who wants to be treated older, but she knew this situation was different.

"Well," Clara began tentatively, "he told me you ran into some people in the woods. I know you've never seen other people so close. Were you scared?"

"No!" Joan quickly spat back at her mother. On seeing Clara's open expression, Joan's head dropped to her chest as she continued. "I mean, they seemed nice, mama. I don't understand why daddy got so upset."

Clara sighed and reached out to grab Joan's hand.

"Daddy was only upset because he loves you, baby. He wants to keep us all safe, we've told you this."

"But you never tell me *anything!* You guys just don't want me to have any fun," Joan whined. Clara's resolve hardened.

"Joan, your father and I have told you all you need to know at your age. We've told you it's dangerous out there and that you can't trust anyone. Your father does a lot to keep us safe and you need to respect his wishes." Clara paused for a moment. "It's going to be a while before we let you off the island again. I suggest you watch your attitude, young lady, if you want the chance again."

Joan glared at her mother, all warmth forgotten.

"I hate you both!" Joan screamed before rushing off through the woods.

Clara sighed as she watched her daughter disappear into the forest. There were only a few hours before dark and she was concerned about Joan being out alone at night. Despite her hesitation, she trusted her daughter to return in time. Rather than go after her, Clara decided to let her go.

* * *

Max paced their cabin while waiting for his family to return. As much as he wanted to go after them, he knew Clara was the more capable of the two of them to calm their spirited child. She had gotten that fire from him, but the bits of sweetness that shone through was all her mother.

The day's events ran through his mind as he walked the worn wooden floors. It had been so long since they saw any people in the area, and he knew he hadn't been as careful as he should have. He'd gotten lazy, compliant. Dark thoughts and scenarios flashed before his eyes, each worse than the last. Before it became too much, he strode over to the door with determination, ready to go after them, when Clara appeared in the clearing. He looked over her shoulder for Joan but Clara shook her head.

"Give her some time, Max. It's been a big day for her."

Reluctantly, he agreed and went back inside to continue his pacing.

An hour later, Joan still hadn't returned and dusk was falling. While both Clara and Max were confident she knew her way around the island, they didn't allow her out alone at night. Large predators were not present on the small piece of land, but there were plenty of other dangers in the dark. Even though FIRE had minimized their ability to feel pain, it didn't mean they couldn't still get hurt.

Grabbing a few torches, they both prepared to go out and look for her. Just as they stepped out the door, Joan emerged into the clearing in front of their cabin. Her head was bowed and a contrite look covered her face. Max and Clara glanced at each other.

"What are you doing, mommy and daddy?" Joan asked sweetly.

"Nothing, baby," Clara replied, looking over to Max with a warning glance. "Come on inside. It's time for dinner."

Max stood in the doorway as his daughter walked by. Her change in demeanor worried him, and he didn't believe for a second she wasn't still angry. Suspicious, but unsure of what the young girl intended, Max followed them inside for dinner.

* * *

Joan snuck out of the cabin late at night, well after full dark. It had taken a long time for her parents to fall asleep and it wasn't until Joan heard her mother's even breaths and her father's light snores that she risked leaving. Usually, she preferred to sleep in her parents' bed, even though she had her own small cot. Tonight, she had asked to sleep alone, saying she wanted space after the day's events. Both her parents seemed suspicious of her attitude but could hardly deny her request. A small part of Joan felt bad for the deception, but this was something she needed to do. To prove to herself as well as her parents.

Bundling her pillow and a few clothes under the blanket, she hoped a cursory glance at the cot wouldn't betray her exit. Earlier in the day, before she had come home for dinner, she had prepared a small bag and grabbed her child-sized spear, placing them inside a hollow log near the eastern shore. She ran down from their home, exhilarated by the nighttime freedom.

The entire time she was doing this, Joan kept her ears open, expecting her father to burst through the trees at any moment. Except for the usual chirping bugs and croaking frogs, all was silent. A grin lit up Joan's face as she realized she had done it!

Thinking back to what her father had shown her earlier that day, Joan carefully unwound the ropes holding their single boat. Holding it still, she placed her bag and spear inside before hopping in and pushing off with the paddles. The reflection off the water was stunning, and every star was visible in the clear night sky. Joan stared upward with wide eyes before beginning her journey across to the mainland. *This will show mom and dad that I am totally old enough to be on the mainland! There isn't anything scary there. Once I come home with some animals from our snares, I know they'll start treating me like a big girl!*

It didn't take more than twenty feet before she realized that paddling alone was going to be harder than she anticipated. She knew that once she got halfway the current would help, but her tiny six-year-old arms strained with effort to keep the boat straight and moving forward. After a warning from her father earlier, she carefully avoided the outcrop of rocks between their island and the far shore. It took much longer than she wanted and she kept expecting her parents to find her gone any minute. Finally, she made it to the current and breathed a sigh of relief as she was able to rest for a moment before the last push to shore.

Chapter 6

Clara woke up disoriented, confused with the remnants of unpleasant dreams running through her mind. She immediately heard Max's soft snores and instinctively reached out to Joan, panicking for a moment before remembering the child had chosen her own bed for the night. Peering over, she could see a small lumpy outline on Joan's cot and breathed a sigh of relief.

Although she tried, she couldn't recall what her dreams had been about and was only left with a disturbed feeling. When her racing heart finally slowed, she got out of bed to get some fresh air. Very quietly, she snuck over to the door and into the clearing outside their home. The moon was full in the sky and Clara raised her face towards it, enjoying the cool calm of the night. It was moments like this she found herself loving where they lived and the soothing quiet, letting the peace envelop her soul.

Feeling better she went back inside, once again opening the door quietly so as not to disturb Max and Joan. As she was closing it, she looked down at the row of shoes she insisted they keep on a mat near the door. Still quite tired she didn't notice anything out of place at first until she had gone a few steps. She looked back, recognizing that one small pair was missing, before her heart began slamming into her chest once more.

Clara rushed over to the small cot, no longer making any attempt at staying quiet. With a trembling hand she pulled the blanket back. *Oh no...*

"Max!"

* * *

Joan hummed softly to herself to dispel the eeriness of the unfamiliar nighttime forest. Everything seemed so different at night, and the vibrant forest of the day before had turned sinister and dark in the absence of the sun. Though the moon was large, the dense trees let very little light through. In the distance, she could hear an owl hooting its late-night post. Small scurries could be heard all around her, and it was only sheer stubbornness that kept her going.

* * *

The hour following the couple discovering Joan was missing was a blur of panic and chaos. Rushing around the dark cabin, they grabbed a few torches and two of their precious flashlights, which they only used in emergencies due to the difficulty in getting batteries. It didn't take them long to run out the door, Clara heading west and Max east.

After about twenty minutes, Max came upon the shore and quickly discovered their boat was missing. He looked out onto the water and far shoreline but couldn't see anything in the limited light of the night. Cursing, he ran back up to the forest where he had a special stash of things for emergencies.

"What are we going to do!" Clara shrieked when Max told her Joan had taken the boat. "I don't know if I can swim that far, Max! Our baby is out there all alone! What if someone hurts her? What if she gets lost!" As she continued, she got more hysterical until Max put her face in his hands, looking into her eyes.

"Clara. Baby. Do you trust me?"

"Yes, of course, but…"

"Then trust me, okay?"

"But…"

"Do you remember when I promised you I would come home? Before FIRE?" Clara's lip quivered as she nodded at him. "Yes," she whispered.

"And I kept that promise, right?"

"Yes," Clara whispered again.

"Well I promise you, Clara. I will get Joan back."

Max held her as she sobbed, his own fear taking a different form. Though he was angry, terrified and worried, this all made him think harder and see more clearly. Panic didn't overwhelm Max, merely focused him. Holding his wife, he began to formulate a plan to go after their daughter.

* * *

Joan was lost. It felt like she had been walking the woods for hours and she still hadn't come upon the snares she had set with her father only the day before. After a while, she realized that even at her slower nighttime pace she should have reached them already. It was then that she decided to turn back, figuring if she headed back toward the shore it would get a bit lighter and she could find them easier in the day. Joan had originally hoped to surprise her parents first thing in the morning with her catch, but knew now that wouldn't happen. She was beginning to lose enthusiasm for this adventure and was wishing she was at home, in bed with her parents.

While Joan had indeed grown up in the forest, she was seldom outside at night, and never alone. She had been so angry, so confident in her own abilities, she never once considered how scary it would be at night. She went as quickly as she dared trying to head back to the beach where she stored the boat.

An hour later and the night was starting to give way to the morning. Faint purple and blue were visible on the horizon, proof of the impending day. She came across the first snare completely by accident. She had stopped at the stream to get a drink when she looked up and recognized it as the place where she and her father had seen the men yesterday. She knew where she was! Rushing onward, she quickly found the first snare trap with a fat rabbit strung up in its grasp. Joan tittered excitedly as she used her small knife to carefully cut the rabbit loose.

"Why looky what we have here!" a voice rang out behind her. Joan stood, frozen by fear, as the three men from before stepped into the clearing.

"Looks like we found a nice little catch!"

"The rabbit looks okay too." Two of the men, Squid and Bear as Joan recalled, laughed heartily while their slow friend Steve stood staring at her. The look in his blank eyes terrified her more than anything.

Joan dropped her hand from the snare and started slowly backing away but was quickly stopped by Squid coming up behind her. The three men circled her.

"Where'd your daddy go, sweetheart?" Squid mocked. Joan finally began to realize the danger she was in and did her best to clear her throat and appear calm.

"He's, umm, just over that way checking another snare. I should go find him." She started to move away again but Bear shot his hand out, grabbing her arm. His hand seemed huge around her thin bicep. He squeezed lightly in warning, causing Joan to whimper.

"I got her," he said gruffly to Squid. "Go check the area."

Without a word, Squid broke off into the forest. Joan didn't notice Steve coming up behind her until she heard sniffling noises in her hair. Letting off a small shriek she jumped away making them laugh. Her heart pounded in her chest and she struggled to breathe. A moment later, Squid came back into the clearing. He looked at Joan with a sinister smile before informing Bear, "Looks like she's all alone."

Chapter 7

Max spent the remainder of the night blowing up the single blow-up dinghy left on the island. Without their regular boat they had no other option other than swimming, which was not something Max wanted to attempt. He had always hoped he'd never need the vibrant yellow life raft he had found on one of his expeditions and cursed himself for not getting a better pump to inflate it.

At first, he had insisted Clara stay behind, saying he couldn't keep them both safe as easily, and besides, what if Joan came back? The high-pitched objections of his wife quickly won out though. She was not about to stay behind while their daughter was missing, and possibly hurt. Clara had taught herself a lot of basic first aid and medicine the past few years using her own memories as well as several books Max had brought. Once upon a time, she had been a nurse, and many of her skills returned quickly when given the additional nudge of reading. He reluctantly agreed it would be a good idea, just in case.

The sun began to rise, a deep red morning that gave the day an ominous presence. Clara had spent her time between looking across the water through the binoculars and packing their backpacks with supplies. Using Ziploc bags, which they had long ago discovered to be useful in transporting and storing things, she packed several days' worth of jerky along with some dried fish and as many first aid supplies as she thought they could manage. While they both hoped to find Joan close to the shore, they knew their daughter's adventurous spirit likely took her further.

Clara paced the shore as Max carried the dinghy down to the water's edge.

Max did his best to appear confident but couldn't resist letting out a whoop when it stayed above water. He grabbed their life jackets and they each took a bag, kissing one another before sliding into the cold Pacific.

Max watched the far shore, trying to decide the best route across. He had one lackluster oar and a second handcrafted one he had given to Clara for her to help steer. It would be slow going until they hit that current. In front of their island was a group of large rocks, not big enough to be considered islands, that rose from the sea at a midway point between their home and the far shore.

On most days Max would avoid going through the center of them, though today he knew they didn't have the time or rowing abilities to skirt the long way around them. Hoping the rocks would be unoccupied at this time of day, they pressed forward.

As they approached, Max could see hundreds of sleek, dark bodies lazing across the rocks. The seals were native to these waters and often used these secluded little places for refuge, a key reason Max tended to avoid them. While they were beautiful creatures from afar, he knew that they were huge animals and could be territorial and defensive. Whispering to Clara to pull in her oar, he let the water slowly drift them through the opening, praying that the seals didn't see them as a threat.

Passing through, Max could feel hundreds of eyes watching them and swallowed deeply. Looking over at his wife he saw her eyes were wide as she watched the creatures.

As they hit the halfway mark, several seals began to snort and toss their heads in their direction. More of them began to do it, elongating their necks in a peculiar head thrust that Max didn't feel good about. They needed to get moving.

Using slow motions, he leaned forward to put Clara's oar back in her hand, indicating for her to slowly put it back into the water. Clara nodded despite the fearful look in her eyes and began carefully dragging the oar through the treacherous channel. Max followed suit and started to edge them away from the islands when one of the larger seals closest to them let out a loud wail before diving into the water in their direction. A dozen more followed directly after it.

"Go!" Max shouted, throwing the silent caution to the wind, and they both began to row in earnest. Before they got much further, a large body scraped against the side of their dinghy, making Clara let off a little shriek. Growling, Max pushed them forward, intent on getting out of the animals' territory. Several more of the creatures began to slap and push against the flimsy raft, rocking it to and fro.

It didn't take long for the seals to turn the raft, plunging Max and Clara into the deep cold water of the Pacific.

* * *

Joan had stopped screaming after Squid hit her, threatening to sew her mouth shut if she didn't stay quiet. The look in his eyes spoke of truth and despite her sincerest desire to stubbornly continue her shouting, she didn't feel confident enough to test these men. Bear had eyed Squid very critically after he hit her but didn't say anything. Joan wasn't confident Bear wouldn't stop Squid from making good on sewing her mouth shut.

As Squid pulled her along through the forest farther from her parents and her home, tears dripped from her face, blending in with the small line of red falling from the corner of her lips. They had been traveling for what seemed like forever to her young mind, but was really only an hour or so. The sun had nearly risen and though the forest no longer had the ominous nighttime atmosphere, Joan was much more frightened than she had been alone in the dark.

As they walked at a fast pace set by Bear, Joan watched as her hard-won rabbit was ripped apart and shared among the men, raw. Although she had tasted raw meat many times before, it was not her preference. Despite her hunger, the way they savagely tore through the small furry body, allowing blood and fur to drip over them, steadily made her appetite diminish.

In addition to taking her rabbit, they had also liberated her backpack and tore through it, taking only the items they deemed useful. The rest they buried near the snare trap before heading on. While nothing was said to her,

Joan got the feeling they were heading somewhere specific. Finally, curiosity overcame her fear.

"Where are we going?" Joan asked them, having learned earlier that asking anything related to the "why" was pointless.

"None of your business, little girl," Squid snarled, squeezing tighter on her arm.

Apparently "what" questions were also out.

"Bear," Squid called ahead, "get me some rope or something. I'm sick of draggin' this kid."

"Get it yerself!" Bear grumbled, still stopping. Squid released her arm and began digging through one of the packs. Free for the moment, Joan looked around with wide eyes, searching for an opportunity to flee. That is, until Steve came up behind her, grinning with a dull yet malicious look on his face. She shuddered before complying, letting Squid tie her wrists together, wrapping the other end to his own worn belt with only a few feet of length between them.

"Keep up," he threatened. "I won't hesitate to drag ya."

The rest of the afternoon, Joan was led by the rope. Luckily their kind didn't tire easily, but even so by midday Joan was beginning to feel weak, having not eaten since the night before. After her second stumble, she finally asked for a break.

"I need to pee, and I'm hungry," Joan complained. For a moment, no one answered her as they kept up their steady march.

"Kid's right," Bear finally replied. "Let's take a quick break." He led them off the trail and towards a nearby stream where they reattached her rope to a log, giving her a few feet slack. Just enough to wash up in the stream and go behind a tree for a semblance of privacy.

With a practiced hand, Bear handed out the dried fish liberated from her backpack. Before handing any to Joan he gave her one warning.

"Listen up, kid. So far you've been pretty good. Keep it up or you'll find yourself getting mighty hungry later, ya hear me?" Joan nodded lightly and took the fish. It tasted of home and she couldn't stop the tears from welling in her eyes.

Now that they had stopped, Joan had a moment to consider her situation. *Mom and dad will have figured out I'm gone by now. They'll probably see the boat is missing. Oh my god, the boat! How will they come find me? No, it doesn't matter. Daddy can do anything. He'll find me. Maybe I can leave clues to help him....* Joan looked around, considering what she had on her—really, nothing but her clothes. *And my barrettes...Daddy got them especially for me, he'd know if he saw one....*

Looking over, she saw that Bear was going through their packs and Squid was wrestling around with Steve. Very slowly, she removed one of her beloved barrettes.

"Hey!" Bear hollered, making Joan jump until she realized he was singling her out. "Time to get moving. We got places to be."

"Where are we going?" Joan asked again as she clutched the hair clip in her hand. This was the first time that any of them had indicated a special destination where they were heading.

"We got some people who will be mighty interested in meeting a special girl like you," Squid grinned at her, malice written on his face.

"W-who?" she asked worriedly.

"Never you mind," Bear snapped. "Let's get a move on." He walked over to untie her rope. *The barrette! He'll see me drop it!*

"Wait!" She cried, "I need to go to the bathroom again." Bear scoffed at her and made an impatient motion for her to get to it.

Circling the back of her tree she went through the motions. Turning towards the trunk, she placed her barrette away from the men right into a small notch in the bark. If her parents could track her this far, they would see the flash of pink and know she was okay. Pulling up her pants, she circled back around with her head held high. Bear eyed her suspiciously for a moment before signaling them all to leave.

* * *

There were a number of things that changed for those who had woken up after their own death at the hands of the FIRE virus. A primary reason for the military experiments that had taken place years ago was to research the reduced pain and temperature receptors of the infected, a side effect that was both a blessing and a curse. While not feeling pain as vividly certainly had its benefits, the reduced nerve recognition of hot and cold meant their kind was very susceptible to both heat stroke and hypothermia. Their bodies simply didn't react to extreme temperatures the way they once did.

Max found himself grateful for this today as he and Clara pushed their bodies to swim the distance to the shore. He was certain that most humans couldn't survive in the frigid ocean waters. Max was also fortunate that the seals, so intent on attacking the brightly coloured and unfamiliar dinghy, allowed them a chance to escape before taking them under too. Looking back, he watched as the last of the raft sank into the ocean.

Clara and Max had long ago re-taught themselves how to swim. The British Columbia wilderness was filled with rivers, lakes, and streams, and particularly once they found their ocean home, swimming had become a necessity. Despite this, though, it wasn't easy going and they still had a ways to go.

They had only been in the water for about fifteen minutes but hadn't covered half the distance to the current. The heavy clothes that they wore for protection further slowed them down.

"Clara," Max gasped as he paused for a moment, "are you okay?" Over the waves, albeit not huge ones, it was difficult to see more than the tip of one another's heads.

"Yes," she responded breathlessly. Though she left the island less often than Max, she was aware of the current they were heading for. She quickly told Max she was fine to keep going and they pushed forward, heading for the current that would help them to shore.

Chapter 8

Joan continued to leave her remaining three barrettes along the path they followed, being careful to ensure that the men didn't see what she was doing. Bear in particular kept giving her strange looks, but didn't appear to have noticed, or she felt sure he would stop her.

By the end of the afternoon, Joan was feeling lonely and defeated. She had faith that her father would find her; after all, he had found her mother from across the country, and she knew he wouldn't rest until he found her too. Still, it had been almost an entire day and there was no hint that they were following at all. Joan thought of every way she could slow them down to give her father time to catch up, taking frequent bathroom breaks and dragging her feet as much as being roped along allowed her. Every time she slowed her pace, Squid would yank on the rope and snap at her to hurry. She contemplated falling or faking an injury but wasn't confident that Squid wouldn't drag her along regardless. Despite his silly name, he was a big man and she didn't doubt he would do it and enjoy every moment.

Joan had asked again where they were going but hadn't gotten any answers, and rather got told promptly to shut up. Any other questions she asked were given the same response and she finally gave up talking or asking anything, despite her deep curiosity of not only where they were going but also the world around them. She had never been so deep into the mainland forest and the plant and wildlife so far from the shore was distinctly different from what she was used to. Deep vivid greens surrounded them everywhere Joan looked, and she marveled at the beauty of the temperate rainforest. When she saw a spiderweb lined with tiny droplets she thought of her mother and became more despondent.

It was still an hour or two before sunset when Bear finally called everyone to stop for the night. Squid tied Joan's wrists to another tree before the three men began preparing camp with a practiced art. Steve wandered into the forest to collect firewood while Bear went through the packs taking inventory.

Squid promptly grabbed a few items—Joan couldn't tell what—then went off into the forest alone. Joan leaned against the tree taking in her surroundings. They were in a small clearing and she could clearly hear water rushing nearby. If she closed her eyes, she could almost imagine she was at home. Tears welled when she thought of her home and how silly she had been to leave. *What was I thinking? Daddy and mommy just wanted to keep me safe and now look at where I am. People are awful. Daddy was right all along.*

Within the hour the sun began to go down and Bear had built a small, nearly smokeless fire. Squid, it seemed, had been fishing and brought several fresh ones back to the camp.

"Hey, kid," Bear said to her. Narrowing her eyes at him she replied, "My name isn't kid, it's Joan." She continued glowering, causing him to bark out a laugh.

"Well, Joan," he answered, "I like your spunk. You were okay today, so thanks for that. I don't much like kids but you ain't bad. Here, we got ya a fish." Squid and Steve watched as Bear handed her one of their freshly liberated fish.

She took it, hesitating for a moment before asking, "Can I cook it?" Squid looked over at Bear, who hadn't taken his eyes off the child. He nodded at Squid, indicating for the man to untie her.

Rubbing her wrists, she tried to give a small smile to Bear before walking over to the edge of the forest. Squid eyed her narrowly but stayed in his place as she grabbed a fork-shaped stick and peeled back some bark before asking for a small knife. Squid laughed at her before being stopped by Bear who gave her one, watching her the entire time with interest as she gutted the small fish and prepared it over the fire.

Everyone sat in silence while they ate their dinner and cleaned up. Bear even let Steve walk her down to the small stream to clean up briefly. Joan wasn't sure what to think of Steve. Her father had told her many times before of a boy named Jay, who had helped him cross the country. He always got sad when he spoke of Jay, but said that even though he didn't speak he was one of the best people he had ever met. Though Steve appeared to be similar in that he couldn't speak, Joan was creeped out by the silent man. She didn't think her father would like Steve.

Bear, on the other hand, seemed to be the leader of this little group. She couldn't quite figure him out either. He didn't give her bad feelings like Squid or even Steve. He was a huge man, and she understood easily where he had gotten the name Bear. It amazed her to look at him, having never seen someone so big before. Even still, he didn't give her the same feeling of unease she got from the others.

And then there was Squid. Joan did not like Squid. His smiles always seemed insincere and every time she hurt herself or was uncomfortable he seemed to relish it. She didn't know what kind of infected he would be in her parents' classes of infected, but she did know he wasn't someone she wanted to be around.

When she came back from the stream, she made a point of sitting closer to Bear than Squid. Joan kept looking over at Bear, quick small glances. This man made her curious. Finally, he seemed to have enough of her quizzical looks and asked what she was doing.

"I've never seen someone so hairy before," she replied smoothly. Even though that wasn't the whole answer, it was true. Her father kept his hair and beard short wherever possible, whereas Bear seemed to have fur more than hair.

Bear guffawed at her comment and even gave her a small smile.

"You're alright, kid," is all he said back to her. For a while longer they sat in silence. It didn't take long for Squid and Steve to curl up in their respective spots around the fire, though Bear didn't seem in a hurry to get to his own. Joan stayed up, hoping to glean some new information about who these men truly were or where they were going.

"Bear," Joan finally said, "why did you take me?" Much to her surprise, he actually seemed to consider her question. Sighing, he rubbed his face before looking at her.

"Listen, kid," he said, and Joan glared at him, making him chuckle. "Alright then, Joan. I don't like taking kids, ya hear? We ain't bad guys, but we work for some bad people, but some of those people do wanna do good." Joan didn't understand and told him as much.

"Whatdya know about FIRE?" he then asked her.

"Well, my mom and dad told me a little about it." She thought for a moment, considering all they had told her. "They said that a lot of people died. And that some of them got up again not dead but different. They brought me here to keep me safe." Joan wrapped her hands around her knees and looked over at Bear, who was staring intently into the fire, listening to her words.

"You know," she told him, happy to be able to finally talk without being told to shut up, "my daddy saved my mommy from some bad people. He came all the way across the country. On a train! After that, they said they came to the forest to keep me safe. I miss them." Bear frowned at her words.

"Kid—I mean, Joan," he asked finally, "how old are you?"

"Six," she replied. He looked up, straight into her eyes. Joan marveled at the depth of them and at the level of feeling she saw looking back at her.

"Thought so," Bear said, almost to himself. "Listen it's time for bed, okay? We got a big day tomorrow."

"Bear?" Joan asked as she began to stand up. "Where are you taking me?" He sighed and rubbed his big hands over his face again.

"Just go to bed, kid."

"Okay."

Despite her tiredness and having not slept the night before, Joan was wide awake for a long time after Bear put out the fire. He had tied the rope to her wrist and then the other end to his ankle, so if she moved, he would feel it. It didn't take long for his heavy snores to fill the clearing.

What if they can't find me? The dark nagging voice in the back of her head cried. *What if they can't get off the island at all because I took the boat?*

Several hours later, her mind finally quieted, and Joan drifted off into an uneasy sleep.

* * *

Once Max and Clara finally crossed the channel, they stopped only briefly to change their clothes and check their supplies had stayed dry. Thankfully, most of their things were kept in backpacks, which had made it across with only one bag lost to the ocean depths. It didn't take them long to find the boat, and they left their soaked layers hanging nearby, not wanting to carry the heavy weight.

Clara had only come across to the mainland a few times a year, if that, and looked into the forest with apprehension. She felt as though she had outgrown any desire for adventure and wished she was back home at their cabin. *Joan wouldn't have gotten far,* Clara reasoned with herself. *In a few hours we'll all be back home.*

Max was very silent throughout the proceedings and Clara had to resist asking pointless questions of what was wrong. She knew how protective he felt over Joan and her and assumed he was blaming himself for her leaving. As much as she wanted to reassure him, she knew it would be useless platitudes.

* * *

While Clara finished hanging their clothes, Max went ahead looking around the ground. He wasn't the best tracker, but had picked up enough over the years. Luckily, the dryness of the summer meant much of the trail would still be visible and he was glad to quickly find Joan's tracks heading south east. *She went back for the snares!* he quickly realized. Not wanting to dwell on it, he went to tell Clara.

The next while was slow going and as much as Max wanted to rush ahead, he was worried he would miss the signs of Joan passing through. He had given Clara his sling and had grabbed his own bow and arrows from their hiding spot near the bank. As well as worrying about losing her trail, Max also knew predators prowled these woods, not to mention the infected men they had met. He hoped they had moved on but his mind kept coming back to their interest in Joan. Gritting his teeth, he ushered Clara forward.

Clara was struggling slightly with the dense forest and stayed a few feet behind Max. He mentioned that he thought Joan had maybe gone for the snares, but it didn't take long for him to realize Joan seemed to have gotten lost. Eventually he saw her small footprints backtracking and felt a small swell of pride. *She realized she was going the wrong way.*

Taking care to follow the trail, he led them back towards the first snare trap.

As they entered the clearing, Max could immediately see that the trap had been sprung yet contained no occupant. He indicated Clara stay on the edge and circled the area, frowning at the picture the tracks were painting for him. Clara watched with apprehension, knowing he found something. She kept silent letting him finish despite the strong desire to ask what was happening. Finally, he made his way back over to her.

"Joan was here," he began. "From what I can tell she got an animal out of the snare, but someone else was here too."

"Do you think it was those men?" Clara asked fearfully.

"Maybe. There are at least three other sets of footprints I can see," he replied, "but whoever it was took Joan with them."

After this discovery, it didn't take long for them to pick up the rest of the trail. Max could see three adult sets of footprints alongside Joan's small ones. There was no way of knowing for sure if it was the infected men, but Max strongly suspected it was.

Max had once considered how unique Joan was, but hadn't thought about it in ages. Their lifestyle left little room for idle thoughts but as he tracked through the forest, he contemplated it. They had met many types of infected before obtaining the solitude they craved but had never met another infected who had seen, or even heard, of one being pregnant. He worried sometimes that Clara would get pregnant again, but with no access to birth control it was a risk they had decided to take. In seven years, it hadn't happened.

Clara was truly a unique case, and while there was the occasional infected child, they were very few. The world of FIRE was no place for children. Max recalled Clara once speculating about Joan's unique circumstance and whether she was the key to a cure for FIRE. A child who was conceived to a healthy woman. A fetus that survived through the FIRE virus and its mother's rebirth and was then born with side effects of the infection, but with no active virus. A child who had all the benefits of the infected, without the brain damage. The idea scared them both, and they had seldom spoken of it since.

As Max was thinking about how bright their daughter is, Clara shouted at him from a short distance behind. Rushing back to her he saw what had caught her attention and chastised himself for missing it. In the center of a large pine tree, a small pink barrette was placed at what would have been a child's eye level. He recognized the clip instantly and recalled how pleased he had been when he found them.

"She's been here," Clara whispered, almost as though afraid the small memento would vanish if she said it too loudly. Max gave Clara a small smile and kissed her forehead.

"We're on the right track, baby. They are only a few hours ahead of us. If we keep up a good pace we can make up most of that difference. We'll find her."

We have to.

As night began to fall, Max took out their flashlights and told Clara they should keep moving. They had found two more barrettes throughout the afternoon, and adrenaline kept them going. With the lights they could keep moving for another hour or so before having to stop or risk losing the trail. They pushed ahead, until eventually Max indicated they needed to stop for the night. As much as it pained Clara, she knew nothing about tracking people in the wilderness and trusted that Max knew best. Without even making a fire they shared a few strips of dried fish between them before curling up together on the hard ground.

It took them a long time to fall asleep, well into the night. They were each plagued with their own horrors and thoughts. Finally, exhaustion overtook them both.

Chapter 9

BANG

  BANG - BANG

  BANG

The sound of gunshots in the distance woke both Max and Clara. It was only barely morning, still as close to night as it was day. They both shot up, looks of horror in their eyes as they realized the sound came from the direction they were heading.

"Joan," they said simultaneously.

Guns were not common anymore; with the difficulty of finding bullets, it had been years since either of them had heard the tell-tale sound. While it wasn't too close, the sound couldn't have been more than a few kilometers away. Grabbing their bags, they ran towards where they had heard the sound. So far, Joan's captors seemed to be taking her southeast and Max no longer felt the need to look for tracks. That just had to be them. Why they hadn't noticed guns when he saw the infected men before seemed irrelevant. The only thing that mattered was getting to Joan.

Max quickly steamed ahead, leaving Clara lagging behind. He was much more used to the rugged forest terrain and knew she wouldn't want him to wait for her. Tears streamed down Clara's face as she ran behind him, willing her body to go faster. Branches tore at her face but she paid them no mind.

After about ten minutes Max stopped, sniffing the air lightly. While not as strong as many predators, their infected state did give them a slightly heightened sense of smell. Turning to Clara all he said was, "Blood." Clara's face whitened as they approached.

Walking into the clearing, they saw the remains of a fire and three men lying dead around it. The smell of blood was strong here, with the underlying scent of the infected and…

"I smell non-infected," Max grimaced as he strode into the clearing. "They were here recently."

He looked down at the first body. *Steve,* he recalled. *These are the men we saw in the forest.* A single bullet had gone directly through his forehead. Seeing this, both Max and Clara rushed around the clearing, but found no small body. The light of the morning was too faint to read any footprints, so Max took a moment to get a closer look at the other men. As much as they were dismayed to not find Joan, at least she wasn't lying among the dead.

The next body Max came across was Squid, who had taken at least two bullets to the chest. Blood still slowly seeped from the wounds, but his eyes remained closed. Max looked down at the man, unsure of what he should be feeling, but was shaken from his reverie by a throaty cough behind him. He rushed over to the third man, Bear, who had also been shot in the chest but was still alive. Despite Max's sincere desire to throttle the man whom he assumed took his daughter, he knew he needed Bear alive if he was going to find out what had happened to Joan. He leaned down next to the large man, pressing a hand to the hole in his chest.

"Clara, come here!" Max shouted. She rushed over immediately, looking to Max for direction. "Will he live?" Bear said nothing but his face paled as Clara knelt to take a closer look. With a practiced hand, she cut away a portion of his shirt to reveal the wound underneath.

"Looks like it went straight through," Clara stated to Max, ignoring the man beneath her. "Is he one of them?" Max nodded tersely, causing Clara to growl before looking back to Bear.

"You'd better start talking, *friend,*" Max threatened.

It didn't take long for Bear to tell them what happened.

"Five of them, came upon us in the night not long before you came," he told them as Clara cleaned his wound, grimacing more out of reflex than actual pain. "Shot my crew, took the girl, left me for dead."

"Why did you take Joan?" Clara asked him, fire in her eyes. "Why did you steal my daughter?" Bear's eyes widened slightly.

"For a good cause, ma'am, I assure you. Besides, we found her wanderin' around," he replied quickly. Max stood over them both, watching. "Listen, Joan told me you guys have been hidin' awhile, that right? On that island?" Max and Clara looked at one another before Max nodded at Bear in confirmation.

"Well, the world's fucked," Bear continued, "but there are still some people who think they can stop this. All of this. Cure the FIRE virus, people like us, once and for all." He groaned as he pulled himself upwards. "Me and Squid and Steve here do odd jobs for all kinds of people. Including some of those who wanna cure FIRE. We tried settling down with some different folks but never got along with anyone, so we've been roamin' for years. When you told us the girl was born with it, we thought she might hold the cure. We was thinking of coming to your island, but she found us first. We was gonna bring her to *them*, see if they can fix this whole thing. I ain't seen a kid that young in years…." He trailed off, deep in thought.

Max was furious as he listened to the man's words. *Was going to come to MY home and STEAL MY DAUGHTER.* Unable to contain his fury any further, he wrapped his hands around the man's neck and watch as his pale face began to turn dark.

"Max!" Clara cried as she wrapped her hands around his, struggling to get him off the now purple man in front of them.

"What, Clara!" Max shouted as he whipped around. Bear huffed on the ground, catching his breath, a hand to his throat as he glowered up at Max.

"We need him!" Clara cried. "If we have any chance of finding Joan or figuring out who took her, we need him *alive*." Max considered her words for a moment, still glaring at the man on the ground in front of them.

"I suppose we do," he finally replied before raising a finger in warning. "For now."

* * *

"Let go of me!" Joan cried as she was dragged through the forest. The man didn't respond and merely grunted, pulling her along. The man holding her was larger than even Bear and was easily the biggest human being she had ever seen, and the darkest skinned. She had never even seen a non-infected this close before and didn't realize they could be such a variety of colours.

"Ahhhhh!" Joan screamed as she thrashed under his arms. While she was obviously worried being with Bear, Squid and Steve, she immediately recognized this group as being much more fearsome. What five non-infected wanted with Joan was beyond her, but knowing the bits she did about her mother's experience left her terrified.

There were four men and one woman, all uninfected. The night before, they had come into the clearing while they slept and shot Joan's captors before taking her. Few words were spoken, and those that had been were hushed so that she couldn't hear.

After her third scream, the one woman turned with a scowl and grabbed Joan's cheeks between her small but tight grip.

"Shut. The fuck. Up," the woman threatened, staring straight into her eyes. Though no explicit threat was spoken, Joan was terrified of the woman and nodded shortly. The woman stared at her a moment longer before dropping her hand and turning, quickly. The man holding her chuckled lightly and whispered, "Bitch," before seeing Joan staring at him and tugging her arm forward.

Other than a brief stop to tie Joan's wrists together, the group made a grueling pace through the wilderness for the rest of the morning with no breaks. Joan wondered if the people realized her parents would be looking for her but, of course, said nothing. *Mom and dad will find me. Mom and dad will find me.* The mantra ran through her head again and again.

After the first hour, Joan calmed enough to get a better look at her new captors in the fresh morning light. The woman, who Joan heard another man refer to as Merritt, had paler skin than the rest that was adorned with small dots. Her hair was orange, tied up under a hat. Joan noted the deep lines in the woman's face that spoke of frequent scowling. Visually Merritt seemed out of place next to the others, who were all large men but gave a similar aura of foreboding. The only other name Joan had caught so far was

Denny, who was the hulking man gripping her arm. His skin was darker than anyone she had ever seen, a deep brown, and it took all Joan had not to stare.

The other three men were similar in build to her father. One of them even had curly brown hair that reminded her of him, another with long blonde hair tied back that wasn't unlike her mother's. The last man she hadn't gotten a good look at and didn't go out of her way to try. He led the group, not looking back once. The only time she really saw his face was when he was standing over Squid, grinning as the infected man bled out. She shivered slightly in recollection. He was a man she had no interest in getting close to.

By midday, the scary man at the front told everyone to stop. Denny quickly pushed Joan towards a tree, telling her to relieve herself if she needed. His dark eyes bore into her, and despite her hesitation, she did as she was told. When she was finished, he pulled her up and added a second rope to tie her to a nearby branch. Joan watched as water bottles and rations were removed from packs. Merritt took a deep drink of her bottle and Joan watched with envy, too scared to ask for her own. *So thirsty...* The woman saw her staring and narrowed her eyes before walking off. Joan lowered her head, feeling terrified, thirsty, and out of place. She didn't see the curly-haired man approach until a water bottle was held in front of her face.

"Here," the man said, holding the bottle out for her, "take it. This one is yours. These guys won't share theirs. Zombie cooties and all." He gave her a small wink and walked away, and she got the feeling he was teasing her. She did remember that word 'zombie' and that her parents had told her it was a derogatory word for people like them. When Joan asked what derogatory meant her mother had smiled lightly and just said it was not a nice thing to call someone who had the FIRE virus.

But what are cooties? she wondered.

"Cam, did you seriously just give the fucking zombie kid your water bottle?" Merritt asked the curly-haired man. He shrugged and replied, "It's my backup one anyway. Besides, if ya'll don't take care of the kid she'll drop before we can get her to the lab." Merritt mumbled something that sounded unpleasant before turning away.

Joan caught Cam's eye and gave him a weak smile, receiving a small head nod in return. The mention of a lab terrified her, but it was good to feel as though at least one person here might be nice to her. *Mommy said something about a lab once....*

Twenty minutes later they were off once more. Other than the water that Cam had given her, Joan hadn't been given any food or anything else. Her stomach grumbled but when Denny untied her and started leading her forward, she said nothing.

* * *

"So, where would these people take her?" Max asked Bear, who was now bandaged and propped against a tree. Despite Clara's hesitance to use her healing supplies, she had done her best to clean the gunshot wound and make him comfortable. Her training wouldn't allow for anything less.

"Well," Bear considered, "Jake was the one who shot me. Mean son-of-a-bitch mercenary that I avoid dealing with whenever possible. He works for what passes for the remaining military outside of Vancouver." Clara paled considerably, praying she was wrong about her assumptions of where Joan was now being taken. She darted a glance over at Max, who kept his face impassive as he questioned Bear.

"What do they do there? What kind of building is it?" Max asked.

"Only been there once," Bear replied. "We avoid the cities as much as we can. The uninfected tend to like to stay closer to what passes for civilization now and aren't too fond of our kind. Big building, though. Been used as a base for years since FIRE's first outbreak. Don't know much about what they do their though other than a few scientists do their work there. They use fancy steam generators so they even have lights and shit. Couldn't pay me to cross into those doors, with the rumors of the experiments those fuckers do. I don't think they'd hurt yer kid though. They'd want to keep her alive if she can cure FIRE."

"What experiments?" Clara blurted, receiving a hard look from Max. Bear eyed her critically for a moment before answering.

"I told you already. They say they tryin' to cure FIRE." Max gave Bear a hard look, prompting him to continue. "But years ago, there was rumors of some other stuff happening there. Met a guy a few years back, called himself Three. Told me some pretty fucked up stuff, but I dunno what of it was true. Guy was a bit of a nut, lives up north somewhere with a pretty black girl."

"Three!" Clara exclaimed. Bear looked at her and a small knowing smile crossed his face.

"Joan told me a bit about ya," he told them. "Sounds like you two had quite a story. Now what I wonder is how a nice lady like yourself got tangled up with that old asshole Three."

Before Clara could reply, Max took her arm leading her away after giving Bear a warning stare. Bear nodded in understanding. He wasn't going anywhere. When they were a safe distance away, but still in sight of Bear, Max turned to Clara.

"I don't think we should tell him," Max whispered. Clara looked into Max's eyes. She trusted her husband and loved him more than life itself. However, she also knew he tended to be overprotective and untrusting.

"Max, he has to be talking about the same place. It's too much of a coincidence. I don't know how to get there, but he does." She nodded towards Bear. "He's a bit rough, but I think we should take him with us. Get him to show us the base. It's our only chance of finding Joan if that is where they are taking her."

Max stared at Clara for a moment. "Go stay with him," he finally said. "I need a minute." Clara nodded and walked back over to Bear, saying nothing.

Max walked towards the nearby stream and sat on a mossy rock. Pulling a barrette from his pocket, he fiddled with it as he pondered their situation.

We are wasting time being here, but we can't go up against five people, especially if they have guns. Clara is right. For now, we have to keep Bear with us and get him to show us the compound. Once we see it, we can figure out a plan. Really, he can't do anything with the information anyway. He seems to not like the uninfected any more than we do. Maybe if we tell him what happened, he'll be on our side. Not that I would ever trust the piece of shit that stole my daughter.

Sighing, Max returned the pink clip to his pocket and walked back over.

Clara and Bear both lifted their eyes and watched him approach as he knelt in front of Bear.

"It all started in a hotel room in Toronto and a fucking doorknob I couldn't open for the life of me," Max began. Bear perked up as he listened to Max and Clara tell their story.

"So it's all fucking true," Bear spat. "Those fucking assholes aren't looking for a cure at all!"

"Well," Clara replied, "I know not everyone there was bad. One of the scientists there, Rachel, helped me escape. She said she was going back there after. I don't think she would have anything to do with that stuff, but it's been a long time," she admitted. Shifting her position, she looked into Bear's pale eyes. Though his scruffy face and demeanor was less than welcoming, she saw something else in his eyes betraying a softness underneath.

"Bear," Clara asked softly, "will you please help us?" Bear let out a laugh, shocking both her and Max momentarily. His face darkened and a grim smile covered it.

"Get revenge on the fuckers that killed my crew, and fucked with our kind? It would be my goddamn pleasure."

Chapter 10

Within the next few hours, tiredness began to overtake Joan. The last few days she'd had no more than a few hours of sleep, and even her durable young body was beginning to feel the effects. She started to stumble over the smallest things, eliciting sharp words from Denny. After the third time, the big man spun around.

"What the fuck, kid! Keep the hell up. This is ridiculous," Denny growled as Joan swayed slightly on her feet.

"She doesn't look so good, man," Cam noted as he took in the girl's stance and the way she was swaying, even standing still.

"She'll live," another voice spat out.

Cam sighed and walked over, picking up the small girl effortlessly. Nodding at Denny, Cam began to walk.

"She's tiny. I'll carry her. Let's go."

Joan wanted to say thank you, show her gratitude, but was asleep before she could utter a word.

Joan woke with a start hours later as she was placed on the hard ground. Opening her eyes, she saw they were in a small cave and that night had fallen. *I slept for the whole afternoon.* She hadn't seen who put her down but assumed it was Cam and made a note to thank him for once again recognizing her struggles. After rubbing her eyes, she squirmed for a moment, hoping someone would let her go to the bathroom soon.

Merritt was building a small fire and two of the men were missing. The blonde man sat nearby, gutting fish in front of him which she assumed they had caught on the way. Her stomach grumbled slightly, and her mouth filled with saliva. *Hopefully they feed me too....*

It didn't take long for the group to settle in. Joan watched quietly, keeping her eyes open for an opportunity to run. As much as she was loathe to go back into the night forest alone, it seemed preferable to whatever these people had in mind.

It was quiet around the fire; the only sounds were the crackle of the flames and the loud rumbles of Joan's belly. Eventually, she was handed a small cooked fish which she practically ate in one bite. While it was far from enough to satisfy her, it did help soothe the loud rumble.

During the setup, Joan had also managed to catch the last few names of her captors. Clark was the blonde one who effectively ignored her, and the man who particularly scared her was Jake, who she was pretty sure was some kind of leader. Jake hardly acknowledged her presence and it wasn't until he stepped away from the fire that she willed the courage to try to find out more, hoping she would have more success than she had with Bear.

"Thank you for the food," Joan said to Clark, the man who had given her the fish. Not even turning to her, he nodded slightly.

"And thank you for the water," she said to Cam, "and for carrying me." In return she got a small but sad smile. She jumped on the small nicety.

"Where are we going?" she asked anyone who would answer. Merritt groaned loudly and got up, walking outside of the cave mumbling something about hating kids. The rest didn't even look at her. Raising her voice slightly, she tried again.

"Where are you taking me?"

Denny turned around at her with hard eyes, making her flinch. "Shut up, kid," is all he said. *Guess they aren't so different,* she thought before curling up on the hard ground and drifting off into an uneasy sleep.

Joan woke to the sounds of chaos and the metallic scent of blood in the air. Barely aware, she opened her eyes to see it was still dark, the small fire only embers. Sitting up with wide eyes she looked across to see clashes and moving bodies. It took her a moment to comprehend what she was seeing. The white skin of an infected became clear and for a moment she thought it was her parents, until she heard inhuman growls coming from their mouths.

"Kid, stay back!" Cam shouted at her, shocking her from her frozen state. She scampered back further into the wall of the cave as she watched madness unfold.

It seemed that a group of infected had stumbled upon them, and her uninfected captors were battling furiously. The ding of metal hitting metal along with the duller thuds of metal hitting body parts made Joan whimper. She held her hands over her ears, remembering the loudness of their weapons from the night before.

Joan watched as one of the infected managed to overpower Merritt, smashing the woman across the face and dazing her before turning its attention to Joan. Her eyes widened in fear as she took in the zombie before her. In that moment, Joan knew this to be the creatures the uninfected were so afraid of. They weren't like her or her parents, or even Bear and his friends. These truly were zombies.

The creature turned on her with a menacing look in its eyes, its mouth wide in a mockery of a smile.

"They have a small one," it cried out as it approached and Joan screamed. It reached with arms outstretched but before it could get to her, a flash of silver rained down from overhead. The creature shrieked as its arm was cut off at the elbow, blood spewing everywhere with small drops, sizzling as it hit the fire. Joan looked up to see Jake's grinning face as he brought the weapon down again, hacking and slashing at the now incapacitated zombie.

Joan heard more screams from further beyond the fire, and squeezed her eyes shut to dispel the horrific visuals from her mind.

Minutes later it was quiet again, and the whoops and hollers of the retreating zombie's signaled her to open her eyes once more. She wasn't sure if she was happy or sad to see all of her captors appeared to be unharmed.

Joan didn't sleep again for the rest of the night.

* * *

On Clara's recommendation, they gave Bear a few more minutes to ready himself before the unlikely trio picked up the trail of the mercenaries who had taken Joan. Despite his automatic dislike of the man, Max found himself impressed by Bear's constitution as he pushed forward even though he had been shot only a few hours prior. Max remembered the heavy feeling, the remnants of pain after having been shot himself in a similar spot almost seven years previously.

They spoke little as they moved through the forest, following the relatively easily laid out trail. The small footprints confirmed they had in fact taken Joan with them and spurred them to move faster. Her captors were only a few hours ahead of them, time they hoped to make up quickly.

When evening finally fell it was Clara who suggested they stop and make camp. Max wanted to continue into the night, but agreed to stop when Clara pointed out that they could lose the trail. Bear had been silent for the last few hours, lost in his own thoughts. Clara told him to sit still while she and Max prepared a fire. Despite the rough man's endurance, she knew he needed to rest if he was going to continue to help them.

It didn't take long for the couple to prepare a fire and get settled. They still had some of their dried food left, enough for perhaps another day for the three of them. Bear only nodded in thanks when Max handed him a few pieces of fish. Grabbing a few containers, Max walked back over to the stream to get more water.

Clara frowned as she watched Bear stare into the fire, absently chewing his food. She didn't know him well, wasn't even sure she particularly liked him, but the expression on his face spoke of something she knew well.

Loss.

Pain.

It was a feeling she didn't think anyone should go through alone. Leaning over, she placed a hand on his arm. Bear looked up at her and the agony in his deep brown eyes broke her heart. She assumed he understood her intent when he sighed and began to speak for the first time in hours.

"I forgot about her," he whispered as tears filled his eyes. Clara looked at him shocked but said nothing.

"The night before you came, I spoke with Joan for a time. Watching her, talking to her. It brought back memories, and all afternoon more bits have been coming back. Shit I never thought I could forget." Bear rubbed his giant hand over his grisly face, heedless of the tears that streaked his cheeks.

"Who did you forget?" Clara whispered back. Bear looked up, misery written all over his face.

"My daughter."

Max entered the clearing, breaking the moment temporarily. Clara got up to help Max for a moment before sitting back down, this time right next to Bear. Max sat across, and knowing his wife's penchant for healing, he left it to her and stayed nearby to provide his own support.

"Tell me about her," Clara asked kindly.

"I don't remember a lot," Bear admitted, a bit calmer now after his confession. "That night after talking to your daugh— to Joan, I dreamed for the first time in I don't know how long. She was in my dream. I don't even know her name, but I remember her face." He gave a small smile and looked up at both her and Max. "She was beautiful, just like Joan. She had dark hair like me. The most amazing smile." Max felt the corner of his mouth curl up, just a little. He knew that feeling of looking at his own daughter, the beauty and joy he felt. Despite his distrust for the man, he could feel and understand his pain. And he remembered that feeling of forgetting, of remembering again. Although Max wanted to not like the man, to curse him for his part in what had happened, he felt his heart crack open just a little and forgiveness begin to seep in.

"I don't know what happened to her," Bear added sadly. "She couldn't have been much older than Joan when FIRE hit. I didn't even remember her when I woke up, never even looked for her." His voice cracked at the end and the big man started to sob, finally lamenting the daughter he hadn't remembered he had. Clara couldn't resist the urge to wrap her tiny arms around him, holding him as he cried into her shoulder. Looking over at Max, he gave her a small nod of approval. She was a healer in every way, and he understood this.

Ten minutes later, Bear finally quieted and wiped his face, giving Clara a slightly embarrassed smile before fire filled his eyes.

"I know you only kept me alive so you could find Joan, find the compound.

But I didn't deserve your mercy. I still don't. When I think of what I would do now if I found out someone had my little girl..." He trailed off again before looking up to both her and Max. "I'm sorry for what I've done to your family. And I promise I will do everything I can to help you save your daughter."

Chapter 11

After the attack on the camp, the pace of the uninfected picked up even more. Though no one spoke directly to Joan, she heard some of them talking about 'zombie' groups in the forests and guessed there were more like the ones she had seen the night before. Joan shuddered when she thought of them, and understood a bit more why people were so afraid of her.

For the next few days they fell into a routine. Dragged along by Denny, the only words spoken to Joan were being told to hurry up and shut up. They moved quickly throughout the days with minimal breaks, and every night Joan would toss and turn as she thought about her parents. As the days went by, her spirit steadily dropped as did her hope in her parents ever finding her.

On the sixth day after being taken by the uninfected, she woke to a different atmosphere than the previous days. An undercurrent of excitement was in the air and she decided to risk asking a question, having figured out that, while she was often told to shut up, the uninfected had yet to actually harm her in any way.

"Why is everyone so happy?" she asked Cam, finding him to be the nicest of the group. He looked down at her for a moment before responding, "Well, kid, we'll be home today."

Joan's heart dropped. "Home?"

Cam nodded. "Yup, home sweet home. Hope you like it. You won't be going anywhere else for a while."

* * *

Max indicated Bear stay still while he and Clara crept up towards the edge of the ridge, staying low to the ground. It had taken the better part of a week, and they were all eager to finally be at their destination. Peering over, Max looked down over the compound they had been looking for. Clara's face whitened even more than her usual pale tone and Max immediately knew it was the same compound she had been kept in years before.

A fence surrounded the entire area, held up in some places by what were obviously post-FIRE repairs. Regardless of the haggard look to it, Max could tell it was a formidable barrier on its own. Barbed wire still covered most of the top and the only entrance visible was a rusty sliding gate which had several people on the opposite side. One of them carried a gun, another an impressive looking bow and arrow set. Several more people circled the building with other various edged weapons. Max's face fell as he recognized there was no way the three of them would be able to get in there. He looked for another moment before crawling back and ushering them both further away from the ridge.

Once they got away Max told them what he had seen.

"It's a suicide mission." Bear shook his head. "I already told y'all I'll do anything I can to help you get Joan back, but it helps no one if we're all dead." Clara dropped her head, feeling defeated. They hadn't come this far to just give up.

"Come up, let's go back and make camp. We can talk more," Max stated, turning and walking without waiting for the others. Before following, Bear crept over to the edge as well and came back to Clara, shaking his head.

They travelled for almost half an hour before making camp, wanting to stay clear of the compound but remain close while they brainstormed.

Wordlessly, the three made camp with a practice borne of the last week of traveling together. They truly made a good team, and Max was beginning to accept that he did in fact like Bear, despite all of his misgivings. Though he had wronged them in the worst way, Max knew he truly regretted it and he also found the man to have many admirable qualities. While he thought of this, he also considered his wife and her own growth over the last week.

Clara had truly loved their quiet island life. Although Max couldn't remember all the details of their pre-infected life, he got the feeling that being a mother and their overall situation had changed her greatly. Over the years he had watched her care for himself and Joan, content with keeping their home. Now, she had a fire in her he couldn't help but find himself attracted to. She never complained about the long hours they walked and in fact pushed them all that much harder. Outside of her comfort zone, Clara had truly flourished. Max had always loved his wife, but this past week of travel helped him gain a whole new respect for her.

Clara caught Max's eye as he watched her start the fire. She gave him a perfect smile, one of his favorite sights in the whole world, and his heart melted. "I love you," he mouthed to her, making her grin grow as she mouthed back "I love you too."

Just then, Bear walked back into the camp with four fish he liberated from a nearby stream. They were all grateful for the incredible bounty their homeland provided. Without it, they would have needed to spend a lot more time daily on hunting and gathering enough food to keep them energized enough to maintain their solid travel schedule.

Max held out his hand to take two of the fish from Bear and they both quickly gutted and speared them while Clara completed the fire. When they were finally all settled, the fish cooking nicely in the coals, they picked up the conversation.

"How are we going to get in there?" Clara asked. "That is the same place I was kept," she told Bear, "but it's been a long time. The only reason we got out before was because of Rachel."

"Well, we don't have any inside help this time," Max responded, stating the obvious.

"One of us could sneak in at night…" Bear began, stopping as both Clara and Max shook their heads.

"Too risky," Max stated. "That fence looks solid, and there is no way they wouldn't see. And as much as you are kind of an asshole who took my daughter, I don't really want you throwing your life away on a half-assed plan." Bear grinned morbidly.

"Almost think you're starting to like me," Bear joked, sending a wink in

Clara's direction causing them all to chuckle lightly.

"Seriously though," Clara said, "we can't do this alone."

Max suddenly perked up, jumping to his feet.

"Guy!"

Bear frowned, "Who's a guy?"

"You mean the guy from the train?" Clara asked, getting a nod in return.

"Remember I told you I took the train, right?" Max said to Bear, who nodded.

"I met some people, infected like us, and they helped me get to Clara, or at least to the right part of the country. They asked me to come with them or meet them after I found Clara. One of them told me where they were going. If we could get there, I am sure they'd help"

"But what about Joan? We have to go now!" Clara gasped.

"How do you know they're still even there?" Bear retorted

Max sighed and gave a small shrug, ignoring the pang in his heart when he thought how close his daughter was. "You said yourself they probably won't hurt Joan. If we go in there by ourselves, we will die. Then Joan will have no one. It's the best plan we have. We can't do this alone."

The rest of the evening they pored over Bear's map as Max tried to recall the areas Sam and Guy had showed him seven years before. Bear did note he knew that somewhere around there was a community, but he tended to avoid those, so he didn't know more than that. Once Max thought he had the area where they got off the train, he was quickly able to get a general idea of where they would be heading.

"Somewhere in here." Max pointed to "Squamish" on the map. "If we leave in the morning, we could be there in two, maybe three days."

They all agreed trying to get help was their best chance and went to their respective sleeping places, all lost in their own thoughts of what the coming days would bring.

* * *

The following morning, the trio headed north with renewed determination and hope. There was no way of knowing if Guy and his people ended up at the place they had intended, but it wasn't a problem worth worrying about now. They had no other options.

They made good time that day and decided to stop early to fish at a small lake they found, hoping to catch enough for a day or two. Max and Bear traded methods with varying degrees of success while Clara wandered the nearby area for edible plants to supplement their diet. She had noticed that the last few days Max had loosened some of his tight control and didn't seem to mind when she wandered, as long as she stayed within shouting distance. She smiled to herself when she thought about how protective he was. Although stifling at times, she knew it was because he loved her.

Taking a deep breath, she marveled at the beauty of the forest that was so like their home, yet so different. Even though she still had a constant worry for Joan, the new scenery and adventure was invigorating in a way she hadn't felt in a long time. *Maybe once we find Joan, I can convince Max to move back to the mainland. I've enjoyed getting to know Bear; maybe there will be more people we can meet, live with....* Clara pondered this as she came upon a large section of blackberry bushes. With a twinge in her heart, she began to collect her daughter's favorite berries.

That night, they feasted on berries, cooking the fish in such a way that they would last a few days. Max even caught a couple of rabbits. The greasy, fresh meat of the rabbits went well with the tangy berries and they all settled around the fire, still feeling upbeat about their current course.

"Tell me about the people from the train," Bear asked as they finished their meal. Max thought for a moment.

"Well, as I said, it was Guy and a woman named Sam who led them. There were maybe twelve or so total, but a few of Clara's friends from the compound planned to head in that direction to meet them. Three was one of them, wonder what changed his mind."

Bear chuckled. "Three's a grumpy old bastard. Not surprised he wasn't into community living." Clara smiled as well.

"It would be amazing to see Seventeen and Three again," she mused, a bit saddened that Bear seemed to think Seventeen was still farther north with

Three.

"No way of knowing who we'll find there." Stretching his arms out, Max let out a big yawn. "I'm off to bed. Goodnight."

Clara and Bear muttered their own goodnights back and continued to sit in companionable silence in front of the dwindling fire. Clara looked up and could see the wheels turning in Bear's head and decided to try for more conversation.

"Tell me about how you met Squid and Steve," she asked, putting her head into her hands. Bear smiled slightly as he recalled their meetings.

"I was by myself for a long time," he began, "never been much of one for other people. Suppose that's why I respected Three so much. It was maybe a year after FIRE when I was shot the first time." He lifted his shirt to show a puckered scar on the left side of his abdomen. "Some rowdy uninfected. Managed to get away, but I was in a bad way. Ended up at a little gas station in the middle of nowhere. Broke in to sleep for the night, get some food. It seemed so quiet and as soon as I bandaged my side, I curled up in one of the aisles and fell asleep. You can imagine my surprise when I woke up and found Steve staring at me, inches from my face." Bear chuckled and Clara smiled. "Son of a bitch had been hanging out there for the whole year alone. I freaked out at first, but then realized he couldn't even talk none. He was wearing this filthy blue uniform, but his name tag was still visible. 'Steve'. When I left, I asked if he wanted to come with me. He didn't answer, of course, but followed along just the same."

"Kind of sounds like how Max met Jay," Clara replied.

"He's the kid who died, right?"

Clara nodded sadly. "I barely knew him, but I've heard many stories. I know Max doesn't like to talk about him much." Bear could understand this, and quickly went back to his story to avoid the unpleasant topic.

"Me and Steve hung out for a few months before we ran into Squid on the coast. We were walkin' through the forest and suddenly heard someone cursing up a storm on a beach up ahead. We crept up and saw Squid throwing a damn hissy fit about some fish that got away. When we figured out he was infected we went and said hi." Pausing, he ran a hand through his copious beard. "Back then, this thing was longer and even more matted. First thing that asshole said to me was, 'Are you a fucking bear or a zombie?' The name stuck, and so did Squid. Three of us were together ever since."

"Sounds like you were really close," Clara commented lightly. Bear smiled sadly and nodded. "Squid was such a dick, and Steve obviously wasn't a great conversationalist, but they were like brothers to me. Annoying brothers, but that's part of family I suppose. Lookin' forward to rippin' apart those fuckers who killed them."

After that, the conversation tapered off and they both let the fire die and went to their beds. Clara curled up next to Max, his strong arms wrapping around her even in his sleep. For so long, it had just been her and her family. As much as she loved them, she was finding herself craving companionship more and more. As she drifted off to sleep, she thought of family, friends, and community. Perhaps when this was all finished, they would find a way to have it all.

Chapter 12

As they had walked through the last bit of forest, the excited mood of her captors only increased her anxiety and Joan's body shook with fear as she was led through the compound gates. She had never seen such a large building! High fences surrounding it, constructed of the strangest looking materials. She immediately felt trapped in, longing for the freedom of the forest. *How will my mommy and daddy find me here?*

Inside the gates were several other uninfected who eyed her warily as she passed. She kept her head down and she didn't pay attention to where they were heading until they approached the entrance. As she was brought through the heavy double doors her eyes widened at the unfamiliar sights and brightness.

What are those lights? Why are they so bright? There are no windows, how is there light! Is the sun up there? Ohmygod, what is this place.... Her mind swam with an overload of new things to process and she began to thrash, her panic finally too much to contain. A moment later, she felt a small pinch on her neck, and everything went dark.

Joan woke with a groan, her body stiff and sore. Opening her eyes slowly, looking through the small slits, she saw it was still light wherever she was. The surface she lay on was cool and hard, and she reached her hand out, feeling the unfamiliar material.

"Are you okay?" a small voice whispered, causing Joan to shoot up. She immediately regretted the decision of moving so quickly and groaned again, her head pounding. Joan opened her eyes a moment later, blinking a few times. *Where am I!*

She looked around and saw she was in a large room unlike anything she had seen before. Ugly metal was everywhere she looked, and she still didn't understand how it was light inside despite the lack of windows. Scanning the room, her eyes finally landed on the owner of the small voice. Looking back at her was a young girl, who Joan guessed was a few years older than herself, sitting in a metal cage adjacent to her own. The girl's pale features were like hers and Joan wondered if she had been affected by the FIRE virus, just like her parents, or was born looking that way, like her.

"Where are we?" Joan asked, a quiver in her voice.

"Compound," the girl replied. "Where were you taken from?"

"What's a compound?"

The girl looked at Joan quizzically. "You aren't from around here, huh?"

Joan shook her head, eliciting a sigh from the other girl.

"Listen, I'm Halee. Doesn't really matter where they took you from, *they* got you now. Compound is where *they* live."

"They?"

"The other people, not like us."

"What are they going to do to us?"

"Well, kid, I don't rightly know. They haven't hurt me really, just poked me and asked me dumb questions. But we aren't getting out of here, I tried. So get comfy, we aren't leaving any time soon."

Joan whimpered, a small pathetic sound. "My mom and dad will come for me."

Halee gave her a sad smile.

"Not here they won't."

* * *

"The child is secure with the other and all relevant parties have been informed, sir," Jake announced.

"Good work, Jake. This will keep them occupied for a while, I am sure."

Jake nodded at his commanding officer, Captain Stephen Cords. "I thought so, sir. As soon as we saw her with those idiots, we knew you'd be pleased.

Any updates from Fort Dearborn?"

Cords shook his head, "Nothing yet, but I am not surprised. You know how communication is these days. I would expect we'll hear from them within the next few weeks, though."

"Instructions in the meantime?"

Cords considered this for a moment.

"For now, stay at base. We have enough specimens for my purposes and the child should keep the rest occupied. Stay close, keep your ear to the ground and be ready."

"Yes, sir."

* * *

For the next two days, Max, Clara and Bear made their way north, skirting the edges of the cities. Though it would take longer to follow the more mountainous areas, they knew that run-ins with other people would slow them more than on the longer route. Cars sat rusted on the roads with yellowed bones scattered throughout the city. The few places they travelled closer to suburbia showed houses being reclaimed by nature. Sagging porches and broken windows with overgrown lawns and a general air of neglect. From afar they looked down on the city. With no lights and a dark sky at night, it was nothing more than a dark blob on the landscape.

A few times they saw signs of fire in the distance, but never went to look closer. The world had changed considerably in the last seven years since the virus struck, but there were still people dotting the now overgrown world. Bear spoke of small communities dotting the coast, both infected and not.

On the morning of the third day they began to see more signs indicating they were close to their destination, Squamish. From the map they could tell it was a decent sized but spread out city. Without better direction, they decided to take the risk of walking through the centre to get a better feel for where a community might be within the area.

Walking down the streets was a first for all of them in many years. The abandoned aura was more prevalent from up close and they all felt on edge.

Much of the pavement was cracked with bits of green popping up throughout, reclaiming what man had taken from Mother Nature. It was strange that despite the desolate appearance, the streets in Squamish were clear of most cars, bones, and other evidence of FIRE that should be present in a city this size. It was simply empty.

"I don't see anyone," Clara whispered after they had travelled a kilometer or two into the dead town. She had spent very little time out and about in the cities at the onset of FIRE but felt as though the desolation here wasn't necessarily the norm.

"Don't mean they ain't there," Bear responded as he scoured the horizon. Max said nothing, his eyes constantly scanning their surroundings. Clara reached out and grabbed his hand for comfort, giving a small squeeze and earning herself a small smile in return. Her mood instantly lifted ever so slightly as they continued.

Once they had gotten to what might be seen as the end of town (beyond was sparser with more farms and homesteads) Max declared they would turn around and walk back again.

Halfway down, the second time, Max spoke quietly without turning his head toward Bear or Clara.

"Don't look around now. We are being followed, act like we don't notice. If it's an ambush they're after, at least we can be prepared if we don't give away that we know." Clara stiffened and tried not to let the fear show on her face. She hadn't gotten wind of anyone in the area but knew Max's senses in this regard to be far superior to her own. Bear said nothing and only gripped his club tighter in his giant paw.

It was only five minutes later when three infected stepped out in front of them, fifty feet away. One had a bow and arrows, the other two with heavy, sharp spears.

"Stop!" One of them shouted. They immediately stopped, keeping a solid grip on their weapons without raising them in an offensive manner.

"We aren't here for trouble," Max shouted back. "I'm going to come closer, I don't mean any harm."

He began to slowly walk towards the trio in front of them when Clara whispered urgently, "Max, behind us." Turning, he saw another four infected behind them. With confidence, Max continued moving forward to the man who had shouted at them. Bear and Clara walked slowly a few feet behind him, Bear watching the other group closely. The group behind them followed, maintaining the distance with their weapons raised.

"Since when do our kind threaten one another?" Max asked as he closed the gap to twenty feet.

"Lot of problems in these parts lately," one of them replied.

Max nodded, "That's fair. As I said, we mean no harm. We are looking for an old friend, told me he would be here. Perhaps you know him."

Suddenly a voice behind them rang out.

"Clara!"

They all whipped around, but only Bear raised his weapon at the light brown woman who was sprinting toward them.

"No," Max told him, putting a hand on his arm. It took only a moment for the recognition hit Clara's face before she too started running forward, enveloping her old friend in a hug.

"I thought I'd never see you again," Seventeen said, speaking into Clara's hair before pulling back and looking into her face. "Look at you! Hardly aged a day, girl!"

Clara smiled. "I've missed you too," she responded honestly, still gripping Seventeen's arm in her hand.

Seeing this reunion, the other infected began to descend upon them with their weapons lowered.

"Appears your friend is still here," one man smiled as he approached. He was an average-sized man with long dark hair pulled back but stood out due to the multitude of piercings and tattoos that covered his skin. His eyes and posture seemed open and kind. "I'm Kenny." He extended a hand toward Max, who returned the gesture.

"I'm Max, this is Bear and Clara," Max replied, "Seventeen, it's nice to see you again. Is Three here? Guy? Are there more of you?"

Seventeen's face darkened slightly. "We patrol the town, but our own place is outside of the city beside a lake. Come on, let's get you back and we can explain everything."

They all headed west out of town with Kenny leading the way. Bear was even more quiet and sullen than usual, which didn't go unnoticed by either Max or Clara. Clara supposed he was no more used to other people than they were but wondered if it was something else bothering him. She made a mental note to ask the man about it later.

"Max," she whispered to him as they walked, "we don't have time for this. We need to go!" Max nodded at her. "I know, but we need help. Just be patient, okay?"

Despite her worry, she trusted Max and gave him a short nod.

No more than fifteen minutes later, Clara, Max, and Bear were shocked to see the community laid out before them. High wooden walls surrounded most of it, with scattered houses and people moving throughout. A lake at one side had small sheds dotting it, with a few larger cabins that Clara guessed had been there prior to FIRE. There had to be well over a hundred people, and that was only what they could see. Fields surrounded much of the commune and they could see animal enclosures with chickens and other livestock running around freely.

"This is amazing," Clara said quietly, getting a small smile from Seventeen. As they approached the main gate, they could see more guards surrounding the top of the walls who immediately opened the large doors. All but Seventeen went back out toward Squamish, leaving Seventeen to guide the trio in. Entering, many people watched them with interest but not contempt. Clara, as well as the others, were shocked to see several non-infected walking among them. The faint smell of the uninfected tickled her nose, but other than being recognizable left her with no other lingering feelings like it did years before.

"Come on," Seventeen said as she led them through with purpose, "Guy will want to see you."

Clara looked at Max. She recalled hearing about Guy and was excited to meet the man that had helped Max get across the country.

* * *

Max was elated to hear that Guy was still around. They headed towards a large tent near the middle of the community. Seventeen asked them to stay outside for a moment, coming out only a minute later to usher them in.

It was dimly lit inside and as they entered, they immediately felt a strange shift in the air. Max noticed Clara's nose twitch lightly and he wondered what her healer's nose was smelling. He blinked a few times to get his eyes accustomed to the lighting before his eyes fell on the bed in front of him.

"It's nice to see you again, Max," Guy said warmly, coughing a bit at the end. Sitting up from the bed, the man swung his legs over and grabbed a wooden cane before standing to greet them. Max smiled as he stepped forward, gripping the man's hand tightly.

"And you," Max replied honestly before turning to his wife, placing a hand at the small of her back. "This is Clara." A hint of something showed on Guy's face as he turned to her.

"Clara. I can't tell you how good it is to meet you. Seventeen told me Max had found you, but I must admit, I didn't think I would ever get the privilege of meeting the woman Max travelled across the country for." Clara's face flushed lightly at the man's kind words as Guy turned to Bear.

"Now, it has been a while, but somehow I don't think Jay has grown up quite this much," he said with a twinkle in his eye. Guy turned to Max and saw his expression, not needing to hear the actual words. "I'm so sorry," He said simply. Max cleared his throat and nodded, swallowing his emotion.

"I'm sorry to say Jay has been gone a long time, but me and Clara owe him a lot. This is Bear, he's a good man and helped us find this place." The big man stepped forward and offered his hand. Max didn't fail to notice the surprised yet pleased expression cross Bear's face at the introduction.

"Good to meet you," Bear said in his low gruff voice as he shook Guy's hand. Just as Max was about to open his mouth to say something else, Guy erupted into a heavy coughing fit. Seventeen moved forward to help the man back into his bed. Max looked to Clara and noted the worried look on her face and wondered if she knew what was wrong with him.

"Now, you must all be tired. We can catch up more later. I have a feeling you aren't just here for a social visit, but for now, why don't you let Seventeen show you around." Seventeen tucked the blanket back over Guy before turning back to them. Max darted a glance at Clara.

"We really can't stay…." Clara began to say but was interrupted.

"You can tell me about it while we walk," Seventeen replied, moving briskly out of the tent. "Come on, I'm sure Sam can help us find a place for you to stay while you are here."

Max was pleased to see that Sam was in fact the same woman he met all those years before. Time had treated her well and he greeted her warmly.

"I can't believe you're here!" Sam gushed when Seventeen brought them over. "Clara, it's so nice to finally meet you. And Bear, lovely to meet you! I can see where you got the name." She winked at the big man who reddened slightly at the lovely woman's attention. Clara chuckled and Max could see the two women getting along well. Just as Clara was opening her mouth to respond, a young boy of about twelve came running up.

"Ma! Joe said you needed me," the boy said as he approached. Sam smiled down and put her arm around the boy.

"Clara, Max, Bear—this is my son, Griffin." Max looked at her quizzically, not recalling anyone so young being with them on the train. "I adopted him shortly after we got here. I run the school now," she told them proudly. Max smiled at the boy. He reminded him of Jay.

"Nice to meet you, Griffin," Max said honestly.

"Griff, you know the empty house by ours? Close to the east field?" The boy nodded. "Can you round up some of the kids and grab some bedding and water and bring it there? We are gonna set these fine folks up with a place to stay." Without responding, the energetic boy ran off.

"Thanks, Sam," Seventeen said. "I'm just going to show them around a bit more. We'll be back soon to get them settled."

It was late in the afternoon, but enough time for Seventeen to give them a brief tour.

"We do communal dinners most nights," she told them as she pointed out the eating area. "Some folks like doing their own smaller meals, but most nights you'll see us all there. We call it the Gathering. Whether it's for food, company or some fun, you're bound to find it there!"

"How many here all together?" Bear asked, finally breaking his silence. Seventeen seemed pleased that he asked.

"At our last count we have one hundred seventy-three infected and thirty-eight non-infected. It fluctuates but has been around two hundred to two hundred and fifty total for the last few years."

"Never thought I'd see a place like this," Max said quietly, the awe evident on his face. Seventeen gave him a questioning look.

"I mean, infected and not living together. Doesn't it cause problems?" Bear and Clara also looked to Seventeen, curious for the answer to a question that had been plaguing them all. It was seldom any of them had met an uninfected who didn't shoot them on sight.

"There were problems at first," Seventeen admitted, "but many of the non-infected here came with friends and family who had the virus. They understand we are just people too. We are the largest mixed community in the area that welcome all types of people, but there are some other small ones around. Occasionally, there are small problems, but to be honest there are more issues among our own people than outside of them." Max's brows furrowed in an unpleasant understanding.

They were all impressed at the level of organization that went into the community. Everyone seemed to have a job, a place to be. It was clean, well laid out, and people seemed genuinely happy.

"We've been raising animals almost since the start," Seventeen told them. "Once we realized the need for protein was greater than livestock could provide, we put more of our efforts into chicken."

"Eggs!" Clara exclaimed as she saw two youth running past with their arms filled with them, receiving a nod in return.

"Yup. That and fish are two of our best sources of protein. We have a few cows and some pigs, but we save those for special occasions."

"Do you hunt?" Bear asked.

"Yes, we have a group that goes out often, especially in the summer months. If you're interested, I can introduce you at the gathering tonight. We eat well, but more food is always welcome. I'm sure we can find a place for all of you."

"We won't be staying," Max told Seventeen, surprising her.

"Not staying! But—but why?"

Clara stepped forward. "Can we go somewhere and talk? I think we should tell you what we've been doing, and why we're here."

The sun was beginning to set in the sky by the time they finished. Bear contributed little, still embarrassed at his own part in what happened. They had all spoken about it before they got here and both Max and Clara assured Bear they would say nothing about his involvement. While both parents still held some resentment, their friendship and understanding grew over the time they travelled together and they both had come to like the man.

"So, she's…*there*?" Seventeen rasped once Clara was finished. Clara nodded sadly.

"We're hoping to get help," she admitted, "but we have to go back regardless. As soon as possible."

Seventeen nodded thoughtfully.

"We've been having problems lately," she replied slowly. "Folks going missing, taken by the non-infected. Mostly the slower ones until a few weeks ago a child got taken outside the fence. You saw the gates at the front? Those used to be open. Since that happened, though, Guy has locked everything up nice and tight. No one allowed to leave except the scout and hunting parties. People are afraid, but don't know what to do about it, and Guy isn't well enough to make the call to action."

Clara grasped Seventeen's arm and looked into her face. "I have to get my daughter back," Clara pleaded.

Seventeen nodded once more. Despite her fear of that place, it was Clara who ensured her own escape so long ago. If Seventeen could help get her daughter back, she would.

"Come on. Gathering is about to start. I need to go get Guy, help him get over. As you probably noticed he isn't as spry as he once was."

"What's wrong with him?" Clara asked curiously. Seventeen gave an uncomfortable shrug.

"He hasn't been well for a while, which is also why we haven't done much about those who've went missing. You've come at a strange time for us, if I'm being honest about it. But I'll let Guy tell you more later. For now, head over there and I'll be right behind."

Chapter 13

Joan and Halee were left alone the few days after Joan was brought to the facility. They had only seen one other person since, another infected man who brought them food once a day. He seemed very unaware of his own surroundings, his movements almost mechanical. When Joan tried to speak to him, he didn't even glance her way or appear to hear her at all. Halee only shrugged when Joan asked about him.

After the initial shock wore off, Joan began to ask Halee more about her life and what the outside world was like. She was fascinated by the descriptions of the community Halee came from and couldn't help but ask a million questions.

"What is 'school'?" Joan asked after Halee finished detailing what a normal day looked like for her back home.

"Some of the stuff you don't know is just weird," Halee teased. Joan stuck her tongue out at the girl, getting a small laugh in return.

"School is like, where they teach you stuff. Our teacher, Sam, is the best. We've been reading this really cool book about…"

Footsteps could be heard tapping down the outside corridor, and both girls immediately looked at each other with concern. It was day three of only seeing the one infected, once a day. He had already come earlier though, and they didn't know what to expect.

As the doors opened, an uninfected woman walked through. Halee seemed to relax slightly, apparently recognizing the woman, but still glared in her direction. The woman had blonde hair and a kind-looking face, though her appearance did nothing to diminish Joan's initial reaction of fear and uncertainty. She carried something flat in her hands that had papers on it, keeping it all tucked under one arm. Closing the door behind her, she made her way toward the cages.

"Hello girls," the woman greeted them. "How are you today?"

Halee growled at the woman, turning her head away. The woman only sighed.

"Hello," she said, turning to Joan, "my name is Michele. I'm a doctor here, and I'm not going to hurt you, as I've also told your friend here. I know your friend can speak rather well, even if she doesn't like to, and I wanted to ask if you could too?"

Joan darted a glance at Halee, who was still glowering at the woman. Turning her attention back to Michele, she inspected the woman closer.

Other than Merritt, whom Joan disliked immensely, she had never seen another uninfected woman before. Michele's hair was a yellow blonde, unlike her mother's pale blonde locks. Her skin was pale, but not as light as her own, and her eyes were a mesmerizing blend of green and hazel. Inside those eyes, Joan still saw kindness. Despite her own instinct, which said Michele was a nice one, she followed Halee's lead and kept her lips pressed together.

Michele didn't seem offended and rather appeared to be interested by her response. Taking out her papers, she scribbled something down. Joan watched with envy as the pen slid across the paper.

"Well," she began, "I know you don't trust me yet, and I can appreciate that. Tomorrow though, we are going to spend more time together and I hope I can earn your trust."

With that, Michele turned and left the room.

The guys who took me would have told her I could talk, right? Why did she ask me that? What was she writing?

Joan turned to Halee, who was still watching the door with unease.

"Who was that?" she whispered. After a small delay, Halee turned to her.

"Some doctor. She asks a lot of questions and stuff. Once in a while, some other people came and took me to another room. They would take my blood and scan my head and stuff." Joan listened to the girl, her eyes growing wider with every passing word. "It didn't really hurt but it all just felt weird."

"W-why would they do that?"

Halee gave her a small smile, more of a smirk.

"We are ex-peer-e-ments," Halee annunciated. "They are trying to cure the FIRE virus."

* * *

Even though it was still early evening, as soon as they left the tent, they could hear the noise from the gathering area and approached to see a lively scene. Long tables were set out and food was being served to some, while others maintained a large fire in the center. People stood around talking and laughing, both infected and not.

Max, Clara, and Bear stood open mouthed for moment, amazed by the sense of community and normality that none of them had witnessed in recent years.

"This is…" Clara began to say.

"Insane," Bear finished for her, causing Seventeen to snort.

"It's something else, all right. Come on, I'll introduce you around. After dinner a lot of us hang by the fire. Sing, tell stories, that kind of thing. That'll be your time to bring up Joan." The three nodded and let Seventeen lead them around.

"Hey guys!" a feminine voice cried out behind them. Sam came strolling up with a smile on her face. "Settling in okay so far?"

"Yes, thank you," Clara responded politely.

"How about you, big man?" Sam teased Bear. He blushed slightly and muttered something about "good." Max smirked at the man's obvious discomfort at Sam's attention.

"Sam," Max interjected, "why don't you show Bear around a bit more? I'm sure he'd love to spend some time with someone so respected in the community." Bear's face was comical with his look of surprise. Sam didn't notice, or didn't care more likely, and quickly ushered him off. As they walked away the words "so nice" and "big and strapping" could be heard from Sam. Max, Clara and Seventeen looked at one another and burst out laughing.

"I don't know if he'll thank you or strangle you later, but either way that was great," Seventeen beamed. "I've been trying to hook Sam up for *years*. Guess a big, burly man is all she needed."

"Hey Sev," a young woman walked up to them. She had light brown skin however, unlike Seventeen, was clearly not infected.

"Hey Abs, what's up?" she replied.

"You told me to find you tonight, so here I am!" the woman responded cheekily.

Seventeen chuckled. "That I did. Max, Clara, this is Abby. She's been with us from the beginning. Guy met her not long after leaving you, as a matter of fact."

Abby's eyes widened. "Max! Guy told me about you! It is so nice to actually meet you! He always wondered if you would show up." Max and Clara both smiled, immediately liking the bright and honest girl.

"It's great to meet you too. Any friend of Guy and Seventeen is a friend of ours," Max replied, putting his arm around Clara who also smiled. Before they could continue, Seventeen asked for a moment and led Abby away. Max and Clara looked at each other.

"Let's walk around a bit more," Max told her. "The more people we can meet the better." Clara nodded her agreement and they continued their wander through the gathering.

After doing another circle, they each grabbed some food and began to look for a place to sit. Just as Clara pointed out a spot, Max's eyes landed on another familiar face. One that also brought back painful pangs of memory. Disregarding the negative emotion, he strode up to the familiar young woman. Curious, Clara followed behind him.

"Cassie?" he asked as he approached. Sure enough, the girl, a young woman now, turned to face him. Her eyes widened in recognition and Max couldn't help but smile.

"M-Max?" Cassie recalled, posing it as a question.

"Yes!" He replied, pleased she remembered and had learned to talk. "You remember me! You've grown up so much." She eyed him for a moment, looking around behind him before asking the question he was dreading but knew was coming.

"J-jay?"

Max shook his head sadly at the girl whose face fell immediately. Before he could say anything further, another infected man approached.

"You okay, Cass?" the man asked her. She nodded her head before burying herself in his chest. The man frowned at Max.

"What is this all about?" he asked, anger evident in his tone. Max looked at Cassie with sadness in his eyes before responding.

"I'm Max. Me and Cassie met a long time ago. She was asking about an old friend. He isn't here anymore. I'm sorry to have upset you, Cassie," Max said. "I am glad to see you're doing okay though." Cassie sniffled but gave Max a small smile. The other man saw this and cooled his confrontational approach.

"Sorry if I came off a bit aggressive there," he told Max. "I've been watching out for Cassie for a long time now. She doesn't speak a lot, as you probably know. I hate to see her upset. My name is Ike." The two men shook hands, sizing one another up. Ike was tall, but lanky, with light brown hair pulled back into a bun. He had a kind face and protective disposition, and Max immediately decided he liked the man. Clara stepped up and offered her own hand.

"Hello Cassie, Ike. I'm Max's wife, Clara."

The four of them spent the rest of the meal chatting amicably. Cassie spoke only a few words and stayed glued to Ike's side, obviously enamored with the man. Max watched her fondly, remembering all too well her own attachment to Jay.

"So, you're the new folks everyone has been talking about," Ike had commented at one point. "Looking forward to hearing your story tonight."

Max and Clara only nodded and continued with lighter pleasantries. They hadn't yet told anyone except Seventeen of their true purpose for coming here and waited for her and Bear to return.

As the night wound down and the younger ones were put to bed, the festivities continued. Ike had told them that while they did have gatherings nightly it was more energetic than usual, and he assumed that their arrival today was being treated as a welcoming celebration. They had lost several people lately, and the excuse to find something good to focus on was just what the community needed. Voices became hushed as Guy made his way onto a small platform. Max couldn't help the small smile that grew on his face at seeing how obviously well respected his old friend was.

"Welcome, my friends!"

The crowd cheered loudly.

"It has been some time since we have had a gathering such as this, and I must say it is so nice to see you fine people enjoying yourselves. You are enjoying yourselves, right?"

Again, the crowd went wild.

"Today, we welcomed three new people, who were known to some of us already. Max, Clara, Bear—thank you for an excuse to celebrate!"

The trio stood and nodded their heads.

"Come up here, please," Guy implored. "I know everyone is curious to hear what brings you here. We could all use a good story." Guy nodded at Max, and he let out a small sigh. He was glad that he appeared to have Guy's support in enlisting help and by the look on his face, Max guessed Seventeen had told him why they were here. Bear grumbled slightly, not liking to be the center of attention, but dutifully followed them to the improvised stage.

The three looked at each other unspeaking before Max cleared his throat and addressed everyone.

"Hello and thank you for having us here. It is a treat for all of us to spend time with you all," Max began, using flattery to win the crowd. Clara smiled and waved lightly. Bear did his best not to scowl.

"Many years ago, I travelled across our great country to find my beautiful wife here, Clara. On that journey, I made a friend who once told me if I ever needed anything to come to him. That was Guy."

Whispers and gossip were quickly drowned out by clapping and murmurs of appreciation for their leader. Some of them had heard a bit of Guy's adventures and even recalled him speaking of the man going after his wife.

"It was in part because of Guy I was able to return to my wife and save her from uninfected who had kept her, and others, as experiments. The place they were kept is only a few days south of here. I understand you all may be aware of this place too, and it's because of this place that we are here now." Max paused, looking over the crowd who had fallen silent at the mention of the dreaded compound.

"Before FIRE took us both, Clara was pregnant. After I saved her, we moved up the coast to raise our daughter in peace. Her name is Joan. Though she looks like us, she was never infected with FIRE."

Instantly, conversations picked up in the crowd. No one had heard of such a thing before. It had been considered common knowledge in recent years that the infected were not able to bear children. Or at least, none of them had known any pregnant infected in all the time since FIRE. This revelation brought questions that had preyed on the minds of many since FIRE.

"Less than two weeks ago, Joan was taken from us." Bear squirmed uneasily beside him. "We followed her captors to the same place that once held my wife." Max looked at Bear, giving him a small nod. He wouldn't tell them. Taking Clara's hand, he turned to the crowd once more.

"We are here for your help. To rise against those who have stolen our daughter from us, and, as we understand, several of your own people. We are here to take a stand against these villains who don't even consider us people. Just *zombies*." He spat out the last word

Angry shouts of approval followed this statement. The word "zombie" was a slur to them, a word that meant they weren't human. While many were content to sit safely behind their walls, there were still many who had lost friends and loved ones who were eager for vengeance.

"We are grateful to you all for taking us in, for hearing us. We won't be staying long, and we hope that some of you will consider helping us. The time is now to stand up for our people." With that, Max leaned toward Guy and shook his hand before making his way back down to their seats.

Many people came to speak with them, both with words of praise as well as criticism.

"You are dooming us all," one man told Max as he approached. Max looked him up and down critically before responding.

"Complacency will doom us all," Max told him. "If we don't stand up now, these people will think that they can do this any time they like. We need to take a stand as human beings, as is our right."

The man glared at Max but said nothing, huffing and walking off.

"That's Lake," Seventeen told Max quietly. "He expects to take over when Guy passes, but many of us don't like him. He can be charming when he wants, but he's selfish and narcissistic." Max nodded, filing the information away for later. He had difficulty containing his anger at the objections he was hearing. The people who thought "well enough" meant leaving their children to be experiments for the uninfected. Luckily, it didn't take long before Seventeen swooped in to take them to their rooms.

After settling them in Seventeen left them, promising to come get them at dawn. The "house" Sam had referred to was just a large two-room shed. There were many similar built around the compound for more temporary accommodations. It suited them fine and was in fact nicer than most of the places they had been sleeping as of late. After a brief conversation, Bear went into his own room.

Max and Clara cleaned up before making their way to their own bed. Curled up in each other's arms, they spoke about the day.

"Max, I'm getting worried," she told him. "They've had Joan for too long. We have to go!"

Max pressed his lips to her forehead. "I know. Tomorrow morning we'll talk to some more people. The next day we leave, whether with others or not. I already promised you, baby, we will get Joan back."

With whispered reassurances and talk of love in her ears, Clara drifted off to sleep.

Max barely slept but stayed still, holding Clara all through the night. Max considered the words of those who were against standing up to the uninfected. He did understand the risk and knew a frontal assault was not the best way to get Joan back. As much as he wanted his daughter back, the thought of knowingly putting people like him in the line of fire was not a pleasant one. Throughout the night he played various scenarios through his mind, each more unlikely as the last. Near morning, he finally fell into an anxious and disturbed sleep.

Chapter 14

Joan had been relatively quiet since Michele's visit, despite all of Halee's attempts to coax her out of her shell. While her parents had kept many things from her, she was a crafty child and had overheard snippets of many conversations. The word "experiment" was one she had heard a few times before, though she didn't quite know what it meant. She did know it had something to do with her mother and what happened to her before daddy found her again. Whenever either of her parents spoke of that time, her mother seemed fearful and uneasy. Whatever an "experiment" was, Joan didn't think it was good and she wanted no part in it.

It was the morning after Michele's visit, and they were expecting their infected waiter to come by with their food at any time. Joan hadn't really felt hungry since she had been here, but on Halee's prompting she ate when food was given. To keep up their strength, Halee told her.

When a familiar clicking noise started coming from down the hall, the girls looked at each other. It seemed Michele, and not their infected waiter, was coming for another visit. A moment later, the blonde woman emerged into the room.

"Good morning, girls," she greeted them.

Neither girl replied.

Michele sighed with a small smile before stepping in front of Joan's enclosure.

"I am going to open your door," she told Joan. "We won't hurt you, but I would like to show you some things. There are guards all down the hall, so please don't run."

With that, Michele opened the door, stepping aside to let Joan out. Joan looked to Halee with fear and apprehension in her eyes but Halee said nothing, though she did indicate with a nod of her head to follow the woman. Swallowing deeply, Joan stepped out of the cage.

For the next two days, Michele came to get Joan once a day. Each time, she was taken to a small room with the strangest objects inside it. Colourful plastics, toys as Michele called them, were all over. Small puzzles, blocks, and even books.

At first, Joan did nothing but stand there taking in the strange sights. With a bit of prompting from Michele, she began to wander the room, touching the contents within. Michele gave her a small smile but said nothing and simply watched. After a few hours, Michele would bring her back to Halee.

Joan told Halee what had happened after the first day and Halee just told her it was part of the experiments. Joan frowned at that, wondering why her mom was making such a big deal about them if that was true. Then she remembered how her father had been right about other people. Since leaving her parents, she hadn't met any nice people except for Halee. Despite her general good feelings around Michele, she was still wary.

On the third day, Michele brought her to a different room. It had soft, cushioned seats like nothing she had seen before and pictures all over the walls. She had seen pictures in books before, but never large displays of art. Her eyes caught sight of a painting of a mother and her child playing on the beach. Her heart clenched and she turned back to Michele, who was looking at her quizzically.

Michele smiled. "Sit, please." She pulled up a chair for herself beside a desk and patted another one of the soft chairs adjacent to it. "I promise I won't hurt you. I just want to talk."

Joan stared at her a moment longer before taking a seat. So far, this woman hadn't harmed her, but she was still keeping her here.

"Thank you. Like I said, I just want to talk." Michele looked at her for a moment, a glint of a smile in her eyes. "I understand you talk quite well. In the report, one of the mercs described you as 'too talky', whatever that means." Now, Michele smiled with sincerity. "I understand you are hesitant, but I truly don't mean you harm in any way. I want to talk to you, teach you some things. And maybe we can help each other."

Joan considered this for a moment. She supposed it was Denny who complained about her. She resisted a smile at the thought that she had bothered the big brute so much. If Michele already knew that she could talk, there really wasn't any harm in her talking. She would just have to watch what she said.

"Okay," is all Joan replied.

Michele beamed at her.

"Very good! See, we will get along just fine." She reached over the desk and grabbed a pile of papers. Joan watched with interest. Her father had brought her paper and books when he could, but for them it had been a luxury.

Michele turned back to her, a few papers in her hands and clutched to her chest.

"Do you have a name?" she asked.

Joan considered for a moment. That seemed safe enough.

"Joan."

"A pretty name for a pretty girl. You already know I'm Michele. It's good to meet you." Michele held her hand out. Joan stared at it a moment. She had never shaken someone's hand before. Michele watched her carefully.

"When you meet a new friend, you put your hand out together and shake them by way of greeting. Would you like to try it?"

Joan thought about it for a moment before nodding, "Okay, but I'm not sure if you are my friend yet."

Michele snorted a laugh, taken aback by the youthful honesty.

"Oh my, well. That is fair, I suppose," she replied still chuckling as she held out her hand for the girl once more.

"Now that we have officially met, is there anything you would like to ask me?"

Joan quickly replied, "Why am I here?"

Michele nodded thoughtfully, "Yes, that is the question, isn't it." She pulled out some of her papers, including something that had a date at the top of it. Joan could see the papers looked quite old, faded and light, and in big letters at the top, it said "FIRE VIRUS HITS CANADA."

Michele handed it to the girl. "Can you read? Do you know what this says?"

Joan stared at the newspaper, her hand shaking slightly. Her parents had always told her about FIRE virus and that it had changed the world, but she had never really seen proof of it. Her parents had been there, and they survived it. Did that mean Michele had too?

"Yes, I can read," she finally replied. Michele nodded again.

"Well, Joan, I don't know what you know about the FIRE virus, but it was a nasty time. Before that, the world was a very different place. And if not for the FIRE virus, we wouldn't be sitting here right now. Do you understand?"

Joan stared at the woman a moment before nodding.

"The FIRE virus does still exist," she explained. "It lays dormant in what we call 'infected' or 'zombies'…"

"I'm not a zombie!" Joan interjected angrily. Michele paled slightly and nodded.

"I'm sorry, Joan. I didn't mean to say you were a zombie. It's a word you will hear though, but I understand why a smart girl like you would think it isn't a nice one."

Joan clenched her jaw together. For a moment, neither of them said anything.

"What is dormant?" Joan finally asked, curiosity getting the better of her.

"Dormant means…asleep. In people who got and survived the initial infection, it is still in their blood and could still infect others, but the virus is sleeping inside them."

"So, what does that mean?" Joan asked, not sure she was understanding.

"Well, it means that people like me are still working to find a cure or a vaccine. A way to keep more people from getting sick," she explained. "And that is why I need your help."

"Why?"

Michele pulled out another piece of paper, all sorts of strange graphs and numbers on it that Joan didn't understand.

"When you were asleep, we took a tiny bit of your blood," Michele told her, "and it showed us something really special." Michele's eyes lit up. "You have very unique DNA, young lady. And you are right, you aren't a zombie at all. You are something else entirely."

Chapter 15

"Wakey wakey!" a singsong voice called out shortly after dawn. Clara groaned and buried her face further into Max's chest.

"You are much too cheery in the morning," Clara complained through the door to Seventeen, who only chuckled. She could hear Bear's door open almost immediately and assumed he must have been up already.

"Come on, babe," Max whispered in her ear, "today is the day we find a way to save Joan. We just have to be patient a few more hours, enjoy the day, make friends. Tomorrow morning, we leave with or without help." With the added prompting, Clara got up swiftly and dressed for the day.

Seventeen led them over to the gathering area once again. Although much more sedated, there were still many people mulling around the area with yawns on their faces. Several people came up to Max and Clara with kind words. A woman named Tonya, mother of the other child that had been taken, was particularly excited to meet them both and had tears in her eyes as she introduced herself.

"I felt so hopeless," Tonya admitted quietly to Clara, "but when I heard Max speaking last night, I felt for the first time since Halee was taken that I might be able to hold my baby again." Clara had hugged the woman and promised she would keep her in the loop of their plans.

A few more people, particularly women, approached Bear with thinly veiled attempts at flirtation, until Sam showed up and led him away to eat with her and Griffin. Though she had eyes only for Max, Clara could understand the rugged appeal of the rough man. Clara smirked as she watched them walk away, pleasantly surprised by the match Sam and he made. She was interrupted by her thoughts when Max spoke.

"Shall we sit?" he asked, a funny tone in his voice as he put out his hand towards a seat. Smiling, Clara accepted and sat down to her breakfast.

* * *

A few moments later, the familiar faces of Abby and Ike approached, followed by a redheaded young woman about the same age who was uninfected.

"Hey guys," Abby greeted them, "mind if we sit with you?"

"Of course," Clara replied kindly, gesturing to the empty seats near their own.

"Hi, I'm Tara," the redhead said. "I really respected what you guys said last night. It's a pleasure to meet you."

"Thanks, Tara," Max replied for both of them, "I am glad to hear our concerns resonated with everyone." He put the emphasis on everyone, making it clear he meant non-infected as well. Tara nodded and they all dug into their food.

As they were finishing up, Abby leaned forward. "I don't know what your plan is, but we would all love to be a part of it." Ike and Tara nodded along. Max looked at Abby, sizing up the small woman.

"Well, we're interested in all the help we can get," Max replied honestly, "but I have to ask, why would you and Tara want to help *zombies* like us?"

Abby's eyes immediately hardened, as did Tara's. Ike leaned back with a small smirk on his face, as though he knew what was about to happen and looked forward to it.

"I don't want to hear none of that 'you and us' crap, you hear me?" Abby quickly and fiercely retorted. "We've been with Ike since the beginning. Most of our friends, they died. Some twice." Tara's mouth hardened but she said nothing.

"Before FIRE, I was a fucking brown homeless girl. I know prejudice, you hear? Y'all are fucking people too. Ike, he is a fucking person. Not a fucking zombie. So now you come here and tell us you want to take a stand against those twisted fucks who think different skin means there is something wrong with ya? Sign us up."

Max watched Abby in a bemused sort of way, while Clara sat there with her mouth open. After a pause, Max stood and held out his hand to Abby.

"That is exactly what we wanted to hear," he told her with a grin.

"Maybe minus all the fucks," Clara added. Silence for a few seconds before the entire group burst out laughing. Just at that moment, Bear and Sam walked up.

"What's so funny?" Sam asked curiously. The group only howled louder.

Once the hilarity died down and breakfast was finished, they noticed Seventeen leaving Guy's tent.

"Max," Clara whispered, pointing towards her. Max nodded and watched as she stepped up to the small stage.

"Good morning all," she greeted the crowd. "Please pass the message along: formal gathering will be at midday. Thank you."

With that, she walked off with a nod at them before heading back to Guy's tent.

Clara turned to Max. "We need to get moving! Joan…" Max held up a hand, stopping her and pulled her aside.

"I know, I know. But if we are going to get help, we need to be patient, okay? I want Joan back as much as you do, but this is bigger than just us now. Just…be patient a little longer, okay?"

Clara's mouth pressed into a thin line, but she nodded briefly. She thought about Tonya, the other woman who had lost her daughter. She didn't like it, but he was right. This was bigger than just their family now.

"Well," Clara began, "looks like we have some time to kill. So…what can I do to help out around here in the meantime?"

Sam perked up at this.

"What can you do?" Sam asked Clara.

"Well, before FIRE I was a nurse. I know a bit about plants and healing and stuff…" Before she could finish, Sam let off an excited whoop.

"Girl, you and me gonna get along just fine! Max, we'll see you later!" Sam shouted as she dragged Clara along. Bear and Max waved them along before turning their attention back to Abby, Tara and Ike.

"Anything for us to do?"

* * *

Sam and Clara chatted mindlessly as Sam led them over toward the medical area. Clara was pleasantly surprised to find out Sam had been an herbalist prior to FIRE and could still recall much of her previous knowledge. Clara wasn't surprised that there was a need for this and was excited to talk about her craft with someone who understood. As they approached, a few people rushed by carrying a young infected man in their arms.

"Out of the way!" Someone shouted, causing Clara and Sam to jump aside as they brought him in.

Once the small crowd parted, they saw that the young man was bleeding profusely, a rag held to his shin which was quickly being coated in blood. The vivid red shone bright against his pale skin.

A slender man walked in, calmly surveying the scene. He had slicked back salt and pepper hair and a condescending sort of strut that immediately put Clara on edge. He looked down at the young man, who wasn't making any noise, but was still sweating profusely and was obviously going into shock.

"Disinfect and clean it up, then grab me some yarrow and we shall wrap it!" The man declared. Several "nurses" began moving to put his direction into action. Behind him, Clara cleared her throat.

"And who are you, madam?" the man asked as he turned to look at her,

"Clara," she responded promptly. "Who are *you?*"

"I'm Terry," the man bristled slightly, as though affronted by the thought that she didn't know who he was. "What do you want?"

"This is Clara," Sam told him. "She's one of the new arrivals."

"I'm a nurse," Clara informed him succinctly. "I'm here to help."

Terry glared at her before his face transformed into a thinly veiled mocking smile.

"What help do you think you can provide?" he asked, making it clear in his tone that he didn't think she would be useful to him. Clara had vague recollections of her time working in hospitals pre-FIRE, and she had a strong feeling she had dealt with such chauvinistic doctors in her past.

"Well," Clara began as she watched others work away at cleaning the wound. Though far from the worst she had seen, he had a solid gash along his shin that had obviously hit a blood vessel based on the amount of blood she was seeing. "If you mix the yarrow with shepherd's purse—you know what that is, right?—then it would be a much more effective way to control the bleeding."

Terry's face went from curiosity to annoyance to open mouthed shock.

"I-I," he stopped to clear his throat, his face reddening slightly, "I think I know my medicines madam! I kindly ask you to leave while I am working!"

Behind Clara, Sam giggled and quickly muffled it with a cough.

"I'll leave you to it then," Clara replied with an exaggerated bow before turning away. As her and Sam left, she heard Terry muttering to someone about finding some shepherd's purse. As soon as they were out of earshot, they both began to giggle.

"I wish we could see his face when he finds out shepherd's purse…"

"Tastes like puke?" Sam finished for her.

Bursting into laughter, they went to find Max and Bear.

* * *

Abby told them there was no time for a proper hunting trip with the meeting at noon, so instead she showed Max and Bear a bit more of the layout of the community and explained more of how they ran things. Ike and Tara left, saying they would see them at the meeting.

"We usually use bows and arrows for hunting," Abby told them as they wandered the edge of the compound. "We have a few people that are really good at crafting them and since wood is obviously a resource we have plenty of, it makes sense. I think you met Kenny, right?"

Max nodded. "Big guy with all the stuff on his face, right?"

"That's right," Abby chuckled. "He looks tough but he's a big softie, really. He also happens to make the best weapons we have, not to mention all sorts of other stuff. He was some kind of child prodigy before FIRE and since then has put all his time into resources and protection."

Max and Bear both looked forward to chatting with him more and told Abby as much.

"Honestly, guys," Abby informed them, "I think most people here are really excited to meet both of you. It has been a while since we had any new faces, and with people disappearing and Guy not doing so well, something feels different here."

"I'm surprised no one did anything before now," Max responded, a hint of anger in his voice. He couldn't understand why people weren't willing to fight for their own people. As this thought when through his head, he realized he had in fact left his own people years ago to take care of Clara and Joan. He had an opportunity, several in fact, to be part of communities such as this and declined in favor of his own family. He realized he really shouldn't judge and decided not to say anything further.

Bear watched Max's face and Max got the impression he understood, at least somewhat, the thoughts he was having. They had grown to know each other quite well during their travels and Max was grateful when Bear changed the subject.

"So, Abby," the big man asked, "I've been hearing a lot about Guy and how he brought so many of you together. How'd you come to meet him and end up here?"

For a moment, Abby's eyes narrowed before she realized he wasn't trying to make a jab about her as an uninfected.

"Well," she replied, "Ike, Tara and me were living in Vancouver when FIRE hit. People called us homeless, street kids, but we had a place to stay. It wasn't much, but it was our home. There were six of us living there and I don't really want to go into detail, if that's okay, but suffice to say it was only the three of us who left. We had a similar plan to you, actually. Grab a boat, head off into the wilderness or find a place. Getting through the city was rough, but we made it. Then we met Guy." She shrugged. "He didn't care that we weren't infected and Ike was. He genuinely wanted to help us. Told us he was heading this way. We agreed, picked up more survivors on the way and seven years later, here we are."

Max smiled at the story. Guy had once offered to take them in too.

Listening to Abby, even with the little he knew of her, he could see why Guy had taken her along. She had a brightness of spirit that hung around her.

"Guy is a good man," is all he said.

"You must have been quite young," Bear commented as he looked the young woman up and down. She chuckled at that.

"I'm not as young as I look," she winked at the big man before answering seriously. "It was just before my twentieth birthday when FIRE happened."

The trio were continuing to walk the perimeter of the community when Sam and Clara found them.

"That was fast," Max commented. He had seen the excitement in Clara's eyes when Sam led her away and was surprised that she was back already.

"Apparently my help wasn't needed," Clara replied with a small smile. Sam smirked behind her and Max wondered what had happened but decided that based on the looks on both women's faces that he wouldn't ask.

The rest of the morning was quite pleasant overall with Sam and Abby introducing them around. While they of course hadn't met everyone, Max could tell that the two women had been strategic in their introductions. All the people they'd met seemed to play a key part in the community and he couldn't help but respect their subtle savvy. It was interesting to see the range of characters living here and how they had come together.

As the sun was almost at its highest point, they all made their way back to the gathering, grabbing a bite to eat while waiting for the meeting to start. As Clara picked at her food, noting the effort put into the delicious meal, she began to feel guilty they had yet to contribute anything. She told herself that once they got Joan back, she would talk to Max about staying, at least for a while, and helping by way of thanks.

The gathering was just as busy as the night before with much of the community nearby waiting for their leader's announcement. They all had some idea of what it would be about but had no idea how Guy would be addressing it. As everyone's curiosity was at its peak, Guy finally hobbled over slowly, using his cane and Seventeen for support, and jumped right into it.

"As you all know, we had some new arrivals yesterday who have asked for our help." Guy nodded in their direction. "You all know that I haven't been well recently, but our missing people, especially young Halee, have been a cause for concern for all of us. Max and Clara's daughter has been taken as well and they are certain it is to the compound south of here. It is safe for us to assume that the others are likely there as well." He paused to clear his throat. "There is a great danger in doing this, but I too believe it to be worth it. If I was able, I would go too, but unfortunately that isn't possible. I will force no one to go, of course. This is a choice each of you have to make for yourselves. Max, could you please come up here?" Max flushed but stood and made his way to Guy, still not used to being around so many people much less speaking in front of them.

"Hello," Max began, "as I said last night, we intend to take a stand against those who have oppressed us, taken our children, our people. Though we always intended to go to save our daughter, the need is so much greater now that we know it is not just her. We understand another young girl named Halee was taken, as well as numerous others who did not have the wits to keep themselves safe. Guy is correct that it will be dangerous, and we will force no one. But we will ask for all the help we can get to save those who have been unjustly taken from us and finally show those people that we will not be pushed around. We don't have a plan yet but are hoping we can work together and figure out the best way for us to accomplish this without the loss of life."

Many people clapped and cheered, but just as many muttered and remained silent. Guy stepped forward once more.

"Thank you, Max. Those interested please go to the west field."

Seventeen came up, having been gone since the morning, to lead them over to the west field where she had set up an area to talk and find out how many would help.

Chapter 16

Within an hour, about thirty people had congregated in their set up space. Max didn't begrudge those who chose not to join them and was grateful for those who did show up.

Among those that showed up were of course Ike, Abby and Tara. Max was pleasantly surprised to see Kenny, the man Abby had spoken about, as well. Sam of course was present, though said she wouldn't be leaving the compound because of Griffin but promised she would do what she could to help see them on their way successfully. Ike made a similar promise, noting he had to stay for Cassie but would help as much as he could. There were several other faces they had met since the night before, including Lake, which surprised Max.

"Thank you all for coming," Clara said, seeing her husband lost in thought. Hearing his wife's voice broke him from his reverie.

"We will never be able to storm the compound with so few," Lake spoke from the back of the group. "What is your plan?" Around him, several others nodded. Though they wanted to help, many were here to find out more before making a final decision.

"I agree," Max told him honestly. "We don't think brute force is the best way. We're fortunate that my lovely wife and several others have in fact been inside the compound. Hopefully, it'll help as we make a plan."

A handful of people grumbled and walked off, not liking the idea that there wasn't even a plan in place yet. Max noted Lake whispering to a few people around him but stayed put. Everyone else waited, seeing what else they would say.

"So," Seventeen stepped up, "here is the map. We haven't been through much of the compound, but this is what I recall." She placed several copies of a rough map down on a table in front of her. Clara looked up at her with surprise but Seventeen only shrugged. "What did you think I was doing all morning?" Clara looked them over and quickly agreed it matched what bits she remembered as well. They hadn't been through much of the compound and when they had, it had been running for their lives. Even still, they did have a vague idea of the building layout at least.

For the next few hours, those remaining got into smaller groups and began talking through various ideas. As the day progressed, the ideas seemed to get worse. As dinner approached, Max was feeling frustrated and defeated. There didn't seem to be any way for them to proceed that wouldn't put them all at a severe risk.

As the others spoke among themselves, Cassie wandered the perimeter of the group. Clara watched as the girl laughed and chased a butterfly, smiling at the small wonder that reminded her of her own daughter. Suddenly, her eyes shot open.

"I know how we can get in!" Clara exclaimed. Everyone turned towards her, eager to hear her idea.

The concept was simple, really. Use the uninfected people's prejudice against them. Since they knew the people had been taking the slower and more dependent infected, they would position a few infected near the compound and present them as such. Appearing to be of the less intelligent variety of infected, they would gain access to the compound by, hypothetically, being captured by them.

"But what if they shoot them on sight?" Tara questioned as she looked worriedly over at Ike.

"How are they going to help people if they are imprisoned too?" another asked. A few people nodded in agreement. It was a big risk.

"What if they weren't just captured, but brought there?" Abby asked. They all turned toward her. "Me, Tara, and any other uninfected we can find. We go there with a few infected as a sort of peace offering. Ask to join them. They would never expect the little girls to be working with the zombies, and then we have more people on the inside and not all of them will be captured."

After working out a few more details, they all agreed it was the best possible plan with the least risk. No matter what they did, they couldn't guarantee things would go their way. But knowing what they did about these people, how they thought and saw the infected, they knew it was their best chance.

Abby, Tara, and another uninfected man named Aaron would be the non-infected side of the equation. Aaron was handsome, strong, and had a field medic background which they assumed would appeal to those who ran the compound. Ike decided to stay behind in favor of staying with Cassie. Since there was a chance Seventeen or Clara might be recognized, they couldn't take the risk to go in as captives. She had told Max about much of what had happened while she was in captivity, and he knew that both of the women would be recognizable if any of the same people from before remained. Bear still hadn't told anyone of his own involvement with the people, and how they might recognize him too, so Max simply told everyone he wanted the strong, capable man on the outside to direct everyone else in his absence. His second, so to speak. Max himself declared he would be one of the ones going in.

In addition to Max, Kenny also agreed to play the part of the captive infected. Max was grateful the smart and resourceful man would be with him, bringing their total to five going in.

Abby, Tara, Aaron, Kenny, and Max.

It was a small number, but they all agreed that any more of them might make their enemies suspicious. Despite their bias against the infected, these were not stupid people running the compound. As well as the five going in, Clara, Seventeen, Tonya, Bear, and three others were all coming, but would remain positioned outside the compound, ready to help as needed. Included in those joining them was Lake, much to everyone's surprise. Seventeen whispered to Max that she expected he thought he would be considered a hero for his sacrifice and they both snorted.

They all went to the gathering for dinner with renewed hope. They had a plan. It wasn't perfect, but it was the best they could do. The next morning, they would start their journey to save Joan, Halee, and the others, and to stand up for their kind.

Many people had already heard about what was going to happen and even those who weren't involved were already giving words of congratulations and thanks for what they were doing. Max, Clara, and Bear had revived something within the community that had been lacking, and people were grateful for that.

It would take them just under two days to get to the compound, with Bear agreeing to take the lead. Guy was very supportive, offering advice on what supplies they might need for the road. Clara found herself really liking the older man and promised she would spend more time with him when they returned. Neither of them voiced any alternative.

At the end of the evening, Max and Clara went back to their temporary home feeling better than they had since Joan was taken, though very eager to get moving. They had been here for two days already and Joan had been gone for almost two weeks. It was time to save their daughter.

"Max?" Clara whispered with a low voice. She was sure he was still awake but wanted to give him an out if he didn't feel like talking. He didn't reply but turned and kissed her forehead in acknowledgement.

"I'm scared," she admitted to him quietly. "I am so scared of going back to that place that I can hardly breathe when I think about it."

"You are so brave, baby," he told her, "and I am here this time. I'll keep you safe." Hearing this, Clara bolted upright.

"It's not me I'm scared for!" she exclaimed. "It's you and Joan. What if you can't get out? What if Joan is hurt? I don't know what I'd do without either of you."

As much as Max wanted to tell her not to worry, that they would both be fine, he knew he couldn't honestly say that. Clutching her closer to him, Max simply gave her the comfort of his love. They both knew there was nothing he could say to alleviate those very real, very justified fears.

Bringing his lips to hers, he spent most of the night showing her body his love and savoring these precious moments with his wife.

* * *

For once, Clara woke with the dawn with no complaints. She and Max said nothing as they dressed and got ready for the day. As soon as they opened their door, Bear exited his room as well and Clara wondered if he had even slept, then blushed as she wondered if it had been their lovemaking that kept him up. That was until she saw Sam exit behind him, a slight redness in her own cheeks as she saw Clara and Max standing there.

"Morning," Bear said, with one of the happiest expressions Clara had ever seen on the rough man's face. She smiled at the two of them, showing her approval before turning back to Max.

"Let's go find Seventeen. It's time." They left Bear and Sam to their own goodbyes as they walked away.

It didn't take long for everyone to gather together. Twelve people total would be leaving for the compound. While it seemed like a small number, they were motivated, and they were fierce. Max and Clara shared their gratitude to each and every one, even Lake, who seemed quite pleased with the recognition.

Clara was particularly pleased that Tonya, the other girl's mother, was joining them too. Tonya's ten-year-old girl had only been taken a few weeks before and Clara saw a familiar fire in the woman's eyes. Clara both understood and respected that look and hoped for the opportunity to get to know the woman better in the coming days.

The entire community seemed to be present to watch their departure, and Clara couldn't help but notice how somber everyone seemed. Gone was the celebratory feel of their mission, replaced by a desolate sense of resolve. Shaking the thought from her mind, Clara pressed forward, eager to go save her daughter.

Chapter 17

After her talk with Michele, Joan's mind was reeling. *"You are something else."* Michele had told her.

What was she then? Right after that announcement, another man had burst into the room demanding Michele's help with something else. Michele had apologized to Joan and taken her back to Halee, promising she would come see her again soon. Halee immediately sensed something was off with the younger girl.

"What happened?" she whispered.

Joan just shook her head. She wasn't in the mood for talking right now. For the rest of the day, Joan refused to speak to Halee. She sat waiting for Michele to return as promised to answer her burning questions.

It wasn't until the next afternoon that Michele finally showed up again. Joan had caved in the middle of the night and spoken to Halee, but still refused to tell her what had happened. She didn't know why, but she felt like Halee would judge her somehow if she knew they weren't as alike as they thought.

* * *

Michele brought her back to the room of toys but told her she didn't have to play, they could just talk if she wanted. Joan immediately began asking questions.

"What did you mean I'm something else?" she asked immediately. Michele nodded in approval at her question. She wanted to take advantage of the girl's curiosity.

"Well, Joan, I told you that the FIRE virus still exists, right? And that some people can still get it from anyone who was infected before? You understood that?"

Joan nodded. "But I wasn't infected before."

Michele looked at Joan a moment, trying to decide her next question, now that her theory was confirmed.

"Joan, can you tell me something?"

The girl hesitated. "What?"

"You said you weren't infected before. Did you parents tell you that?"

Joan said nothing, a slight widening of her eyes betraying her fear of speaking of her parents to this woman. Michele watched her, not surprised by her refusal to respond. She had suspicions about where this girl had come from.

"Joan, were you born like this?"

Again, Joan said nothing.

Michele sighed. "Would it help if I told you why I was asking these questions? That's fair. Well, Joan, when we tested your blood, we didn't find any sign of the virus being dormant in your body. You look very much like those that have been infected by FIRE. The time we have spent together has shown me that you have many other similarities, including your ability to metabolize protein and the effects of temperature. Despite that though, I believe you when you say you weren't infected with the FIRE virus. Based on how old you look, I would say that you were born with all of the advantages, effects, and appearances, but never experienced the actual virus."

Joan face went through a range of emotions as Michelle spoke, ending somewhere on a confused sort of acceptance.

"So?"

Michele watched her carefully as she continued, "Joan, I don't know how much you know about how babies are made, but you know that you need one man and one woman to make a baby, right?"

Joan nodded.

"Well, one of the lesser known effects of the FIRE virus is that people who have had it can't seem to have babies anymore, and we actually don't know why. This is one of the reasons you see very few zom—people who have been infected who are young, like you. Your friend downstairs would have been very young when she was infected, something not many children live through. You, however, are different. I think somehow, your parents had you after they were infected, or you wouldn't be this way." Michelle paused a moment to let that sink in.

"Joan, I believe that because of how unique you are, your DNA and blood could be the key to not only a vaccine, protection for people like me, but also a cure for the FIRE virus. And if I am right, you could possibly even help a cured infected be able to have children. Joan, you could help a lot of people."

After Michele shared these thoughts, she could see the girl was closing up and changed the subject. They chatted for much of the rest of the afternoon. Seeing how interested the girl was in the world, Michele wondered where she had grown up to be so naïve about so many things. Deciding to be as open as possible to encourage the girl to do the same, Michele told her all about the world before FIRE. She found the girl to be bright and inquisitive, and despite her goal to try to remain neutral, she found herself becoming very fond of the tiny zombie.

"Well, Joan, I have enjoyed talking with you today."

Joan smiled shyly. "Thanks, Michele. I mean, for telling me so much stuff. No one ever tells me anything so, thanks."

"Who won't tell you anything?"

Joan huffed, "My parents. They say it isn't important and I need to focus on 'now'."

"Are you parents still around?"

Joan stilled immediately, obviously realizing what she had said. Though Michele had hinted at it, Joan hadn't yet acknowledged her parents before now. Sensing her panic, Michele changed the subject quickly.

"It's okay, Joan. I should take you downstairs now anyway. We can talk more about how you can help us tomorrow." Michele paused for a moment. "I know the place you are staying isn't very nice right now. I have tried to ask some of the soldiers, the people who run this place, to move you girls, but they have said no. Is there anything I can bring to make you more comfortable?"

Joan considered this for a moment.

"It gets boring in there. Could me and Halee have some books or something?"

So, the other girl's name is Halee, Michelle thought without saying anything. Smiling, she quickly agreed to see what she could do.

Michele paced her tiny office after Joan left as she considered her next steps. So far, the child had been very receptive. Much more so than the other girl.

Halee, Michele recalled.

For the last three years, Michele had been effectively running the sciences department here, with her focus being primarily on a cure. Over the years, limited and slow lines of communication had been opened among the last strands of humanity. All over North America there were groups of varying sizes, both infected and uninfected, with several facilities similar to the one they still occupied in Abbotsford, British Columbia. Theirs was the only one like it that they knew of along the west coast, though, and had advantages that few others did, such as renewable energy. They were also one of the few who had any data from the original infection and the virologists studying it seven years ago. They had much more than scraps. They had Rachel Samborski's data, and Michele Samborski intended to finish the work her sister started.

When the facility was first being used, Rachel had been one of the first to discover the intelligence of certain "zombies." Not only that, but she was the only doctor anyone had heard of who had an encounter with a pregnant infected. Unfortunately, the data was all from the first trimester, so there was no way to know if that infected ever carried to term. Even still, her research combined with later findings of the infertility of the infected had Michele fascinated.

Before the FIRE virus, the Samborski sisters both went into the sciences. Rachel, the older of the two, had ended up as a world-renowned virologist. Michele, however, went into anthropology as a passion of hers, but felt like she was always playing second fiddle to Rachel. Despite this, she looked up to and envied her older sister.

Michele arrived at the compound five years earlier, after the sisters connected through the Network after many years, Michele threw herself into Rachel's research: working towards a cure and a vaccine for the virus. The sisters spoke at length about how fast humans could die out if only the uninfected were capable of reproducing; there simply weren't enough people and still far too many risks with the less intelligent uninfected.

Part of Rachel's theory was that her cure would not only help with the urgent need of the infected for protein, but also help the more intelligent infected be able to reproduce. The problem was, however, that they so far hadn't found any obvious medical reason for the infected to not be able to reproduce. It just didn't happen. This was a concept they had not relayed to those in charge of the compound, simply telling them they were looking for the vaccine.

When Michele first heard Rachel's theories she had scoffed; that was, until she met Nikki.

Nikki was a zombie.

Not only that, but she was one of Rachel's researchers and had been infected while studying the virus. Michele arrived at the compound just days before Nikki was infected, turning a week later. Over the course of several months, Rachel proved rehabilitation of the infected was indeed possible with Nikki. Nikki helped with the research and was the key to the creation of a test that would show immunity. Unfortunately, they had yet to be able to use the immunity gene towards any vaccine, but at least they knew which people not to station where they would be at a higher risk of infection. Unfortunately, Michele herself was not immune, but refused to put aside her work even knowing the risks. Ever since, Nikki had stayed in the compound, assisting Michele with the continuation of Rachel's research.

Many of the soldiers and others within the compound were wary of her, and she readily agreed to staying in her own space. She was intelligent with a fierce streak and didn't much care for the prejudice of others.

"I can think, walk, and do pretty much anything in circles around those jerks. Let 'em be scared of me," Nikki would say before mock biting the air. The first time, Michele admitted she jumped back, but had quickly grown fond of the odd undead woman.

Three years earlier, when Rachel died in a freak accident within the compound, Nikki and Michele had continued her work as best as they could. Unfortunately, many of the onsite staff had other projects to work on and the two women were often left on their own as far as vaccine research went. Finally, Captain Cords officially assigned the rest of the staff to various other projects. People simply didn't think there was a point any longer.

"So, you really think this little girl is it, huh?" Nikki asked Michele as she continued to pace. Michele nodded.

"She was definitely born with it. I already told you I suspected as much, and she pretty well confirmed it. She doesn't want to talk about her parents though, that much is obvious. I think they're still alive."

Nikki considered this for a moment.

"I saw her when they brought her in. She looks young enough for it. Do you really think it could be the child from that woman?"

"It's the only documented case we know of. And even if the mother left the area, she probably stayed within the province. Nikki, I think it is. She's also smart as hell, way smarter than most kids her age."

"You know once Cords finds out about what we're doing he's going to try to stop it hard and fast."

"That's why we need to keep it quiet and try to get the girl's cooperation as quickly as possible. If we want to be able to work on this, her agreeing will make things significantly easier. And it's going to take time to do the tests we need and synthesize the vaccine. I don't think I can force or harm a child, even for that."

"Well, perhaps I should go meet the girl then."

* * *

Joan and Halee were chatting when they heard footsteps down the corridor. Pausing, they looked towards the door and both widened their eyes in shock when a beautiful infected woman entered the room holding a pile of books. The woman had long, dark hair that accented her pale infected skin. She was tall, lithe, and pretty, and though her smile seemed sincere, it put both girls on edge. The only other infected they had seen so far other than each other was their waiter, who was incredibly lifeless even compared to many of the simpler infected.

"Hello girls," Nikki said, smiling as she stood in front of them. "My name is Nikki. I was told you might like some books to read in here."

The girls eyed each other warily. Nikki smiled at this and let out a small cackle.

"I'm not gonna bite, girls. I'm just here to bring you books. Which one of you is Joan?" she asked.

Joan narrowed her eyes a bit but knew that Michele had likely told everyone she talked by now. She raised her hand ever so slightly but said nothing.

"Ahh, hello Joan. It is nice to meet you." Nikki turned to Halee. "Would you care to share your name, sweetie?" Halee growled at the condescending woman, eliciting a light laugh from her.

"Fair enough," is all Nikki said. Breaking the books up into two piles, she slid one into each girl's cell before sitting cross legged in front of them with another.

"Would you like it if I read to you?" she asked, holding up the book in her hand.

Once again, the girls looked at each other. After a moment, Joan turned to the woman and nodded. Smiling, Nikki opened the book.

Chapter 18

Bear led the way out of the community and towards the compound. They made good progress, everyone feeling refreshed and eager to move, and by nightfall they determined they would likely arrive at a similar time the next day.

Tonya and Clara chatted amicably throughout the day, veering off the subject of their missing daughters and focusing more on past events and anecdotes.

Tonya was shocked when Clara told her she had been pregnant with Joan when she was infected, and for the first time Clara confirmed her suspicions about those infected not being able to procreate. Or at least, she had another large test group indicating it wasn't possible. Clara prayed those within the compound never found out the truth behind Joan's birth. While she always knew that Joan was likely unique, she hadn't realized that no other infected anyone had heard of had given birth after contracting the virus.

Tonya told Clara about her own turning and how Halee and she both contracted the virus when the young girl was only four. They had spent months on their own before meeting a few other infected and eventually making their way here. Clara was amazed they had been able to survive on their own for so long, knowing what she did now about the state of the world at the time, and her respect for Tonya soared.

Tonya had been telling Clara a story about remembering Christmas for the first time and the celebration she held for Halee, when Max declared it was time to stop for the night. Clara rushed over to pull him aside.

"I was right," Clara said. "No one has heard of anyone infected with FIRE having given birth or gotten pregnant." Max listened with his lips pinched. "Rachel told me if people ever got a hold of me that she didn't know what they would do. What if they find out about Joan? Max, we need to keep moving."

Max looked at her before gazing over at the rest of the group. Catching Bear's eye, he nodded the man over.

"Would we be able to keep traveling at night?" Max asked the man without preamble. Bear considered it for only a second before shaking his head.

"Not a chance. The forest is dense and its way too dry for torches. I'm likely to get us lost in the dark, anyhow."

Clara listened with a pained expression. "But…"

"Clara," Max interrupted, a sympathetic look on his face, "we can't do it. You were the one who stopped us in those first days when I wanted to keep going, remember? I know how worried you are, baby, I know how much worse it is the closer we get. But if we get hurt or lost it won't help Joan. We can wake up at first light and try to move fast. We'll be there tomorrow." Bear put a hand on Clara's shoulder as she sniffled.

"We'll be there tomorrow night. We'll get your little girl."

Chapter 19

"You sent *her* in with them?" Captain Cords admonished. Michele scoffed.

"I don't know what your hang up is, Stephen. She's more than proven herself trustworthy over the years."

Cords grunted in response, sitting back in his chair. His head was pounding already before the doctor had come in with her updates and just thinking about the tiny zombies in their possession right now just made it worse.

"I don't like it," he finally replied.

"I told you, it is the best way to get the girls trust. We don't have the resources or people to be able to force her cooperation, and the results could be skewed if we try. I opened the doors, Nikki can lead them through. We *need* cooperation if we are going to get anything out of this."

Cords eyed her critically for a moment and was about to open his mouth when someone started frantically banging on the door.

Sighing he yelled out, "Come in!"

One of the outside guards burst in the doors.

"Sir, thought you'd want to see this. Three folks just showed up asking to join up with us," the man said through huffed breath.

"You know the rules. Only if they have one of the relevant backgrounds," he responded sharply.

"That ain't all, sir. They got a couple zombies with 'em."

* * *

Max stared at the ground, doing his best not to twitch at the discomfort of the blood coating his shirt as he tried to play the part of mindless zombie. Both him and Kenny were tied at the wrists, the other end held by Aaron, who was standing with a foul expression on his face, his stance wide.

"What's takin' so long?" Abby complained to the guards in front of them. Tara tapped her foot impatiently behind.

It was early evening when they arrived and they decided to approach the compound right away. The rest of the group was spread around the area in pairs, keeping watch and staying at the ready.

"We don't usually let random folks in," one man answered.

"Pretty girls, however…" another sneered.

Aaron grunted and glared at the man, who feigned a cough and turned away. Both Abby and Tara smirked and tossed a grateful smile at Aaron.

The doors behind them opened and another man walked out. Though he was dressed in the same faded army fatigues, he held an air of confidence about him that the others didn't. He was quite tall with dark blonde hair dotted with bits of silver. He was a handsome but severe-looking man, and in seeing his approach, Abby straightened up.

"What's all this about?" the man said without preamble, gesturing to Max and Kenny.

"And who might you be, wanting to know?" Abby asked sweetly, only a hint of condensation. The man smirked at her.

"Anyone ever told you that you got balls, girl?"

"Yes, sir. Many times. Big brown ones," Abby responded glibly with a straight face.

The man burst out laughing as the guards mulled around, unsure of how to react to the unprecedented outburst.

"I like this one," the man said. "Take them to my office. Put the zombies with the others." He turned on his heel and began to walk away with the confidence of a man who knew his orders would be followed.

"You never told us your name," Abby shouted after him.

"Captain Stephen Cords." He stopped for a moment, a smile in his voice, before continuing.

With no other option, they followed.

Everyone did their best not to react as they walked into the lit building. While the base was by no means at full capacity, the solar and turbine power generators had been kept up well over the years. None of them had seen artificial light in a long time.

As they walked in the doors, Cords turned on his heels and the two men standing there immediately stood up straighter. Max watched out of his eyelashes, keeping his gaze low. He wanted to learn as much as possible about the people running this place and the layout.

"Until after our 'talk', I'm going to ask you to hand these gentlemen any weapons on your persons," Cords declared with a small smile. Abby narrowed her eyes for a moment before returning a tense smile.

"I don't like it, but that's fair I suppose," she replied, nodding at Aaron and Tara. "I assume you are promising us safe passage through your place regardless of taking us in, ya?"

Cords' smile broadened before he gave a small bow.

"Of course," he replied. "Take these two downstairs, room B."

* * *

Max and Kenny shuffled behind the two soldiers, making their way down the long corridor. Through the corner of his eye, he watched which hallway and door Abby, Tara, and Aaron had followed Captain Cords into. For effect, he let off a small moan.

To his surprise, the men leading them weren't pulling them hard or mocking them. Rather, they treated the job as though it were completely beneath them. They just didn't care that they were dragging along a couple of zombies. Max couldn't help but wonder how many times they repeated this act, and his growl picked up in earnest.

One of the men flicked his eyes back, frowning at Max, before pushing open a set of doors. A foul smell wafted up from the stairs below and Max tensed. As they continued down, a few faint moans could be heart and Max couldn't help but look up.

The room they were in had a large cage with around ten infected mulling around inside. None were children, and Max instinctively knew that this was the same place that once held his dear wife. His fists tightened in an effort not to react.

"Come on then," one of the men said in a bored tone as he stepped forward and opened the door to the cage. Kenny shuffled forward entering the room followed closely by Max before the door shut behind them and they were left alone with the other infected.

Kenny immediately looked around at the ceiling before giving the thumbs up to Max. No recording equipment he could see. Kenny walked over to the group, who were mulling around and didn't seem to notice they had just gained two more members.

"Dude, it's me, Kenny. You can stop pretending," Kenny said to one of the men. The man stared at him with a glazed look in his eyes, causing Kenny to frown before turning back to Max.

"Something is up," Kenny told him. "Bill was one of us. He went missing months ago, but I don't think anyone ever connected it with this place. He can speak just fine."

"Can any of you speak?" Max asked the group. Two of the infected looked up briefly, but the glazed look in their eyes proved they were not all there. The men looked at each other for a moment.

"They must have done…something," Kenny said, still frowning. Letting out a sigh, he turned his attention to the cage they had been put in, particularly the lock.

"It looks pretty solid, but I'm pretty sure I can pick the lock given a bit of time. It will damage it visibly though, so I won't do it until you are sure we are done here and are good to go, okay?"

Max nodded. He hoped to find out more about this place first, but also didn't know how that would happen if they were in this cage. That a previously intelligent infected now was acting differently worried him even more, but there was nothing he could do with that now.

"What do you think?" Kenny asked.

"Well, I don't know how we're going to find Joan or the others from here, but I think we should hang tight for a bit until the others come back with more information."

Kenny gave a small smile, putting a hand on Max's back.

"They'll do their part, don't worry."

* * *

Nikki read them a story called The Ugly Duckling. Despite herself, Joan found tears running down her face at the small animal's plight. When she had been taken here, she was the ugly little goose among the ducks of the uninfected. Maybe one day she would find her beautiful goose parents again.

"So, girls, did you like the story?"

Joan nodded and Halee had stopped growling, but neither said anything. As Nikki began to get up to leave, Halee stopped her.

"Why do you help them?" Halee burst out. With her back to the girls, Nikki smiled, schooling her face to empathetic and neutral before turning around.

"Because I want to help people who helped me," Nikki told them. "I was a scientist when I turned and these people saved me, kept me here and safe."

Joan frowned. She didn't know why, but the more time she spent around Nikki, the more off she felt about the woman. Nikki just didn't give her the same sincere feeling Michele did.

"Don't you want to be safe and happy?" Nikki asked the girl, essentially ignoring Joan. Halee seemed to consider this.

"I guess so…"

"Of course you do!" Nikki interrupted. "And if you girls help us, then we can make sure everyone is safe and happy." She paused a moment. "What is your name, sweetie?"

Halee froze but quickly warmed up, apparently not feeling as threatened by the woman who was one of them. "Halee."

"Halee. What a pretty name. How old are you, Halee?"

Halee paused a moment, and in that time Joan willed her not to answer. She didn't know why, but she didn't trust this woman.

"Ten," Halee replied.

"Well, Halee. I have to go now, but maybe later we can talk more, okay?"

Halee gave a small smile.

"Okay."

Once Nikki's footsteps faded into the distance, Joan turned to Halee.

"I thought you hated people?"

Halee shrugged. "She's one of us."

Joan huffed. "If she was one of us, she'd let us out."

Turning her back to Halee, she grabbed one of the books and began to read.

* * *

Nikki dropped her smile the second she exited the room. Truthfully, she couldn't stand children. She knew how to play her parts though, all of them. She walked into Michele's office, where the woman was sitting at her desk with papers spread out everywhere.

"I got the other one to talk," Nikki told her. "Confirmed her name was Halee and that she isn't the same age as Joan, she's ten."

Michelle smiled, "You were right about her warming up to someone who looked like her faster. How was Joan?"

"She wasn't as open to me. Damn kid cried when I read the ugly duckling. I think you're best with what you've been doing. She seems to like you."

Michele nodded.

"Well, we confirmed what the tests did. The other girl, Halee, isn't needed. I wonder if we should separate them. Put Halee with the others, give her the serum. Joan may cozy up to me more if she's alone."

Nikki nodded. "When are you going to try?"

"I should do it as soon as possible."

"And Cords?"

Michele scoffed. "The idiot doesn't need to know. Just tell him the one girl isn't working out. As far as he is concerned, our sole purpose is the vaccine."

Nikki's jaw tightened, but Michele didn't notice.

After leaving Michele, Nikki wasted no time in heading down to Captain

Cords' office. She smirked at the guards, who gave her a wide berth, and even chomped her teeth at one while laughing.

Knocking once, she entered the office where Cords had three people in front of him. Nikki stared a moment at the two women, one dark skinned with brown curly hair and the other almost as pale as her but with fiery orange hair. They all looked back at Nikki with wide eyes.

"Ahh, Nikki. Why don't you welcome our newest recruits? This is Abby, Tara, and Aaron," Cords blustered. Giving a small smile, Nikki walked around the desk to stand beside Cords.

"Hello," she greeted them simply.

"Officer Yards?" Stephen called out to the guard outside his door. A middle-aged man entered the room, saluting his captain.

"Please escort these three to their bunks. Area C should have some space for them. Show them where the mess hall is on the way then report back to me immediately."

"Yes, sir."

Standing, Abby thanked Cords before motioning Aaron and Tara to follow the officer down the hall. Once they left, Nikki closed and locked the door, turning to Cords.

His eyes narrowed at her.

"You shouldn't be in here," he warned her. Nikki let out a light laugh.

"Oh, Stephen, you worry too much."

Sighing, he rubbed his temple.

"What do you want, Nikki?"

She smiled. "It's almost time. Samborski will be taking the child any day now. She's separating them first. If we want to keep her from moving forward, you need to act soon."

Chapter 20

Sam hummed to herself as she prepared dinner for Griffin and herself. Although they often went to the community gatherings, she tried to make sure they ate with just the two of them at least once a week. As she put on the final touches, she thought about Bear for the dozenth time that day. Would he join them for dinner one day? The image of family was a strong and pleasant one in her mind.

The night before everyone had left for the compound, she and Bear had spent the night together. Though she hadn't been celibate in the years since FIRE, she couldn't remember having felt so strongly about a man. After he left, she vowed to herself that she would tell him how she felt when he returned. If he returned. She pushed that thought from her mind.

As she was about to call for Griffin, she saw him running towards her, his face red with exertion.

"Ma, you gotta come. Brian and Sarah just got back. There's a problem."

Sam rushed towards the gathering, unnerved by the impromptu visit by some of their favorite drifters. Sarah and Brian were an infected couple who dropped in on them usually a few times a year. Not belonging, or wanting to belong, to any one group, they traveled around visiting the various communities set up throughout the West coast. Drifters helped pass messages and information and were well accepted into most communities. There were several small groups like them, but Sam was particularly fond of these two. They had only visited two months prior and weren't expected back until after the winter.

Slowing down as she approached, she saw the couple sipping water with a group of people around them. Brian caught Sam's eye and gave her a nod in acknowledgment.

"Sam, good to see you again," Sarah greeted her.

"And you. What brings you guys back so fast? Griffin said there was trouble?"

The couple both nodded.

"Sadly, I think there might be," Sarah replied.

"We had just stopped by the place in Bellingham for about a week, and I went to do a final fishing trip before we headed out. That is when I saw them," Brian told her, with Sarah nodding along.

"There is a group of uninfected coming north, and based on what a few inside sources told us, they are coming this way," Sarah picked up.

"How many?" Sam asked.

"At least fifty but probably more," she replied. "But we couldn't get close enough to count exactly."

"We followed them for a day," Brian continued. "They go pretty slow having to stick to main roads. But they are heading to the compound, I'm pretty sure."

Sam frowned as she took in this information.

"That's not all," Sarah told her. "When we were in Bellingham, they told us about a few places further south. Some of the military are finally banding together and have already taken out at least two communities that we know of. At first it was just the angry ones that have been roaming around, but it seems they have finally decided we are all still a threat."

"Sam, we think they're trying to wipe us out."

Sam paced her and Griffin's living area, thinking over what she had been told. Based on what Brian and Sarah saw, they expected the others to arrive at the compound within about three days. Sam thought of all her friends who were, hypothetically, there now. She thought of Bear.

She had to warn them. If she ran, she could be there a day ahead of the others.

Not wasting another moment, she went to speak to Guy and make the arrangements.

* * *

Clara fidgeted, waiting for Tonya to hand her back their one set of binoculars.

"May I?" she asked for the third time, holding out her hand. Tonya's mouth was pressed in a thin line as she reluctantly handed them back before going to sit with the others. Though Clara was obviously worried too, Tonya was not handling the stress of being here very well despite all their attempts to calm her. The night prior she had been crying out in her sleep and Seventeen was now sporting a black eye for her efforts in waking the woman.

"This is ridiculous," Lake whined behind her. "What is going on down there? For all we know they've all been captured."

Clara put down the binoculars for a moment and rubbed her temples. Every day since they arrived Lake had been whining and complaining, and she was sick of it.

"No one's asking you to stay," Seventeen replied coldly. Lake turned up his nose with a small huff before walking to the other side of the clearing. Clara heard a small laugh from Tonya and smiled before turning back to the compound.

In the waning light, Clara peered down the valley into the expansive compound below. As before, there were half a dozen soldiers milling around inside the compound gates, but nothing else moved. Sighing, she wandered back over.

Seventeen gave her a small, encouraging smile and patted the spot beside her.

"How you holdin' up, girl?" Seventeen asked her.

"This is driving me nuts, Sev. I can't stand sitting around here waiting."

Seventeen looked at her sympathetically.

"I know, but right now this is all we can do. Be here and be vigilant. You don't know Abby and the rest well, but they are all solid. I have no doubts that they will get Joan out of there. We just gotta be here and ready when they do."

Clara nodded miserably but said nothing.

As Seventeen left, Bear came over to take her spot. The two sat in comfortable silence for several minutes.

"Do you think people can change?" Bear finally asked Clara, breaking her from her melancholy. She thought about this a moment. She had certainly changed since they left home. She knew Max had changed since FIRE and everything that happened to them.

"Yes," she finally answered decisively, "I do."

Bear just nodded.

"Why do you ask?"

He sighed and rubbed his large hand over his scruffy face. Clara waited patiently for him to speak.

"I really like Sam," he admitted quietly. Clara fought to hide a small smile.

"Is that a bad thing?"

"Well, not for me, no. But for Sam."

At this Clara frowned.

"I forgot my own kid," Bear said with wetness in his eyes. "I made bad decisions about working for the wrong people and because of that, my team, my brothers, died on my watch. I'm no good for anyone."

"That's ridiculous," Clara declared. "Do you know how many people forgot when they woke up? I remember what it was like too. If things had been different, I may not have remembered Max either. And you can't blame yourself for your friends' death, Bear. It was other people, not you. You can't blame yourself for FIRE or for the actions of others, it'll eat you up inside if you do." Clara paused to take a breath and swallow before finishing quietly, "And as far as trusting the wrong people, what you did, you did because you thought it could bring a cure for all of us. If Max and I can forgive you then you should too."

Bear sat silently for a few moments before responding.

"I'd been with Squid and Steve for years and before that, I was alone. The night before we left, Sam hinted about me stayin' but I didn't say anything back. I don't know anything about community livin'. And I definitely don't know nothing about how to treat a beautiful lady like that." He sighed again and this time Clara smiled for real.

"You know," she told Bear, "after Max saved me, I had a tough choice to make. Three and Seventeen and all our friends asked us to come with them, but Max wanted just me. And you know what? As much as I knew nothing about living alone or in the forest, and as much as I would miss my friends, I chose Max. Do you want to know why?"

"Why?" Bear asked curiously.

"Because he completes me. And when I am with him, nothing else matters." Clara smiled as she hugged her legs, just thinking about her husband giving her warm butterflies. "If you care about Sam and she cares about you, nothing else matters."

Chapter 21

Michele came to visit the girls again the next morning. Halee peered behind the woman, seemingly looking for Nikki, before scowling and turning her back to Michele.

Joan couldn't help but notice how tired Michele looked today and wondered what was going on outside of this room. She still held out hope that her parents were coming for her, but it waned with each passing day. After the fight with Halee when Nikki left, Joan was beginning to feel like Michele was her only friend in the world.

"How are you doing today, Joan? How about you, Halee? It was so nice to learn your name, I would love it if we could talk too."

Halee didn't respond, of course. Joan rolled her eyes at her friend and stood up.

"I'm okay, Michele," Joan told the woman as she waited for her to unlock the cage. Stepping out, she followed Michele down the hall without a backwards glance.

"I thought today we could go talk some more."

"I would like that!" Joan responded enthusiastically. She loved hearing more about the world and about FIRE. Plus, Michele said she could help people like her parents. She wanted to help.

Michele gave her a small smile.

"Tomorrow, though, we will be doing something different. I want to talk to you about that and make sure you understand and still want to help, okay?"

Joan nodded as she followed Michele into her office.

* * *

A few hours later and Joan's mind was reeling as she was led back to her cage. She understood a bit better what "experiment" meant now, and why Michele wanted her cooperation. She wanted Joan to stay here for a long time.

"Now, most of it won't hurt, Joan, but some might be uncomfortable or boring. But it will take time. As I told you, I have two goals and I think you can help me with both a cure and a vaccine. A lot of it won't make sense, but I will need to do things like biopsies, take blood, and all sorts of other tests for my experiments...."

All this swum around in Joan's head, but truly the only things she heard were "bones," "blood," and the dreaded word, "experiment."

All Michele wanted her for was an experiment. Her parents would never find her, and she would have to stay here forever being poked and prodded by people who didn't care about her. Joan didn't care about a cure, she wasn't sick, and neither were her parents. She just wanted to go home. Joan vowed to make up with Halee as soon as she was back. At least she could have one friend.

Her heart felt heavy as the soldier opened the door to the room; Michele hadn't even walked her back. Joan's eyes widened as she took in the empty cage next to hears.

"Where is Halee?" Joan asked the man as she began to panic. He merely grunted and pushed her forward. Tears ran down Joan's face as the man slid the lock back into place and left.

Curling up in the corner of her cage, she hugged her knees and sobbed.

"Daddy, where are you...."

* * *

Max hadn't been able to sleep all night, despite Kenny's advice to get rest while he can. They didn't know what the coming days would bring and they would need their strength, Kenny had told him. But Max couldn't settle. He was so close to Joan, his baby girl, and he was locked in this damn cage. He paced the cage for hours, weaving in and out of the infected that were with them. Kenny had spent some time trying to get others to talk, but none had been able to respond. They talked again about what could have happened to the previously able to speak infected, but neither man could do more than vaguely speculate.

The morning after they arrived a few soldiers had brought them some buckets of food and water. Max looked down at them with disgust, the half-rotten fish and meat holding no appeal. Drinking a bit of water, he sat against the back of the cage and finally closed his eyes. While he didn't intend to sleep, he must have drifted off because the next thing he knew he was awakened by the sound of steps from down the hall.

He and Kenny caught each other's eyes a moment before resuming their acting just in time for the doors to open. Noting the other infected were drawn by the noise, they both looked up to see a large, dark skinned soldier dragging a young girl slightly older than Joan by the arm. Another man followed with a set of keys.

"Come on," the man growled at her. The other opened the cage while the dark-skinned man all but tossed the small girl in. As soon as they left, Kenny rushed over to the girl.

"Halee, are you okay?" he asked the girl who was still sprawled on the ground. Max quickly joined them. Opening her eyes, the girl looked up at Kenny with a blank stare, blinking once before sitting up.

"Halee?" Kenny said, the tone of worry evident in his voice. She stared forward blankly, not even acknowledging that he had spoken.

"Let me guess, she was like us too?" Max asked, even more worried now. Kenny nodded, his brow furrowed as he watched the girl wander over to the bucket and grab a handful of meat. Like the others, she ate it quickly and began to wander about the cage. After watching this for a moment, Max walked up to the girl and took her by the shoulders, leaning down to look her in the eyes.

"Halee, have you seen my daughter? Have you seen Joan?" When the girl didn't respond, Max growled in frustration.

"What are these people doing to us!" he cried out, Kenny quickly shushing him. Max let his legs slide down as he sat against the back wall.

The need to find his daughter was an all-consuming one. He didn't know how much longer he could stay in this cage before he went crazy, and it hadn't even been a full day.

Abby, you better have a plan and you better get it moving, soon....

Chapter 22

Abby and Tara walked close together as they headed toward the mess hall. The night before they had been shown around a few basic areas of the base, but only the few places they were expected to go, such as the barracks and cafeteria. Abby hoped to have more time to look around today, but for now she and Tara needed to blend in as much as possible.

Walking into the cafeteria they were unhappy but not shocked to see there were only a handful of women among dozens of men. They both did their best to ignore the leers and stares as they walked up to the line to grab their food. With trays in hand, they turned to look for a place to sit. A man with curly brown hair caught Tara's eye after a moment, giving her a gentle smile and indicating the empty seats next to him. The smile seemed sincere, and with decision, Tara nodded to Abby and the girls went and took their seats next to him.

"Thanks," Tara said to the man, holding her hand out. "Tara." He took it and gave it a firm shake before turning to Abby.

"Abby," she said, slightly less friendly than Tara but still polite.

"Hey, I'm Cam. And no problem, I know some of these jerks get weird around pretty women. They'll get used to you soon."

Both girls nodded and gratefully dug into their food without further conversation. When they finished, the girls both got up to wipe off their trays before they were interrupted by Cam.

"What's your duties for the day?" he asked them, following behind.

"We need to go for assignments," Tara told him. "Could you show us where to go?"

Tara and Cam chatted amicably as he led them towards the assignment office with Abby following just slightly behind. She had a pretty good idea of what Tara was doing and had to admit, it was a good idea. Tara had always been a sexual sort of girl. With her pale skin, freckles plus long ginger hair, she was a striking woman. The years of living like they did had firmed and shaped her young body, and Tara knew it. Abby did her best not to smirk, letting Tara work her magic.

They hadn't seen Aaron since earlier but knew his background as a doctor had gotten him in with the medical crew. Abby hoped he would have a chance to find out more about what they were doing with the infected here, or at least where they kept them. Tara got assigned outside with Cam, while Abby got an assignment inside. Watching the two walk outside, still chatting happily, Abby let her mask drop as she made her way towards her assigned area. This was her chance to look around, and she could easily blame wandering into random areas on being new. If she could stay out of sight, she might get a better idea of the compound layout.

Walking briskly at just short of a jog, she rushed away from the main areas, doing her best to recall the map Seventeen had shown her. Unfortunately, she and Clara hadn't seen the entire base and had left in a bit of a rush, so Abby didn't know much. Abby had a fantastic memory for direction, though, and was confident that with the little bit she knew, she could make some educated guesses on where they might keep a bunch of zombies.

Abby turned down a hallway and paused in her tracks as a tall, female zombie exited a door at the end of the hall. With wide eyes, she watched the woman lock the door and turn towards her before Abby realized it was the infected she had seen in Cords' office the day before. *Nikki*, she recalled.

"Why hello, little soldier girl," Nikki greeted her mockingly as she approached. Abby did her best to remain aloof and said nothing, continuing to walk forward. Nikki shot her hand out and grabbed Abby's arm, causing her to panic slightly.

"Let go," Abby quickly spat out, trying to wrench her arm free.

Nikki laughed. "I don't think so, little girl. Nothing for you down here. Come, I'll show you where to go."

With that, Nikki led her away. Abby gritted her teeth at the woman's grip on her arm, having always had an aversion to people she didn't know touching her.

At her assigned post, Abby couldn't see any easy way to get away. She had been assigned with a large man named Denny who had leered and chuckled at her when she introduced herself. As Abby stood there, bored out of her mind, she thought of the woman zombie, Nikki.

Abby had always prided herself on her instincts. Before FIRE, she had been homeless for years and more than once it was her gut feelings that had saved her ass. And for whatever reason, she got a bad feeling about Nikki. What was an infected doing walking around? And why had the woman steered her away from that hallway so fast? As soon as she could get away, Abby was determined to answer those questions.

* * *

Aaron was fortunate that he was considered a valuable commodity to Captain Cords, being both a soldier and a medic. He had been informed that he would be accompanying some other groups in the near future on scavenging missions, but for now was to get a feel for the base.

"Aaron, right?" A woman came up to him. Though it was now worn down and slightly stained, the once-white coat she wore told him she was also some kind of medic or nurse.

"Yes, ma'am, that is me," Aaron responded pleasantly, putting down the research papers he had been given to look through.

"I want you with Private Yards. Time to do a dose of serums on the two new ones so I want someone with a bit of a physical background with him." The woman turned to walk away.

"Serum?" Aaron asked her. *Serum for what?* The woman waved his question off and kept moving.

"Yards will fill you in," she shouted behind her as the man Aaron assumed was Private Yards approached with a black pouch in hand.

"Private Phil Yards," he said, holding out his hand in greeting.

"Aaron," he replied, returning the shake. "So, what are we doing?"

"Administering the serum," Yards told him. "Come on, let's get this over with." Aaron frowned but followed the man.

"What's the serum?" he asked. Yards stopped and looked at him a moment before snapping his fingers.

"Oh yeah, I forgot you're new here," he chuckled. "So, every zombie in our compound gets this," Yards explained. "It's an injection that keeps 'em nice and docile but keeps some intelligence so they are receptive to basic orders. We're still working on perfecting it, a lot of them just turn plain stupid. But at least they don't bite and shit"

Aaron did his best not to react, keeping his movements slow and precise until they finally approached a door where he stopped Yards. His mind was racing trying to make sense of what this would mean for all of them, but especially Kenny and Max.

"Is it permanent?" Aaron asked him, praying it wasn't. He had a feeling the 'new' ones the woman had spoken about were Max and Kenny, and his brain raced with ways to stall this.

"Nah, we have to re-dose them every so often, but only first time is an injection."

"How often?"

"Depends," Yards told him. "Some of the little ones can go close to a week, but we usually do it every three days in their food and water." Yards began to step forward but again, Aaron stopped him.

"What's in it?" Aaron asked. This time, Yards frowned at him.

"You ask too many questions," Yards responded critically. "Come on, let's get this over with."

Swallowing deeply, Aaron followed him into the room where, sure enough, there was a cage full of infected. He saw that not only were Max and Kenny among them, but also several others he recognized, including Halee. His face paled as he watched Yards open the gate to the cage. Not one infected moved forward or even looked at them, though Aaron could tell both Kenny and Max were watching subtly.

"Come on," Yards called impatiently as he approached Kenny while Aaron stepped into the cage.

"Hold this one, they sometimes thrash a bit when you first inject 'em," Yards told him as he grabbed Kenny's arm. Knowing there was nothing else he could do in this moment, and much to his own shame, Aaron helped Yards inject both Max and Kenny.

Aaron watched as the awareness faded from both of their eyes and as he followed Yards out of the room. He looked back once and saw both men now standing around with the others and he let one small tear slip from his eye.

He needed to find Abby and Tara, now.

* * *

Abby picked at her food at dinner, her shoulders slumped over. The day seemed to have lasted forever, and she was convinced if she had to do another shift with that asshole Denny that she might stab him. As she began to picture the various ways she could disembowel the unpleasant man, she didn't notice Aaron approaching until he sat down across from her.

"Hey," he said nonchalantly. Abby looked up to return the greeting but paused when she saw the look in his eyes betraying the friendly tone.

"Hey yourself," she replied belatedly. "How was your day?" She knew that he wouldn't be able to tell her anything but hoped he may be able to subtly divulge a bit of what was bothering him.

"It was okay," he replied as he picked at his own plate. "Dosed some zombies with the serum." Abby tried not to let her eyes widen. She hadn't heard anything about this serum, but she knew Aaron well enough to know that it wasn't good.

"Cool, I was just on guard duty. Tara's still on, outside I think," she told him as she finished her last bite. Standing up, she took on a more flirtatious stance and walked around behind him. She knew others were watching, and what people assumed of women like her. Leaning down, she whispered in his ear.

"Come over later," before winking and walking away. Aaron smiled and a few whoops and hollers came from the men sitting around the table. One even slapped him on the back.

As she left the room, Abby let her face drop. Hopefully that would give them a good excuse to talk. She didn't know where Tara actually was, but assumed she was still with Cam and that she'd see her tonight in their shared quarters.

It didn't take long for Aaron to join Abby. Though the base did separate by gender, as long as people weren't on duty, they encouraged casual liaisons. Not nearly as many women as men had ended up at the base, and repopulation was on everyone's mind. Putting a sock on the doorknob, the universal "gettin' busy" symbol of the past, Aaron pushed the door shut and sat on the bed beside Abby, dropping his head into his hands.

"Tell me," Abby said without preamble.

"They're dosing them with some serum shit," Aaron told her without lifting his head. "It makes them stupid, docile. They are using them, or want to at least."

"What do you mean, using them?"

Aaron lifted his face, which was now streaked with tears. He opened his mouth once as his voice cracked and Abby's heart dropped. Her and Aaron had known each other a long time and she had never seen him like this. After a moment, he took a breath and tried again.

"I don't know Abs, but they made me give it to Max and Kenny. And I saw…" he choked up again and Abby wrapped her arms around him. Aaron composed himself after a moment.

"Abs, Halee was there too. And Bill, and I think a few others. They're all…dumb." Aaron tried to hold in his misery, "And I gave it to Max and Kenny. Abby, it was like they weren't there at all. I watched the light leave their eyes. I shouldn't have done it but I didn't know what to do! I neutered my friends, for fucks sakes!"

Abby listened, her eyes wide and her brain running on overdrive.

"It isn't permanent," he told her after a moment. "They do it every few days. I'm gonna have to go back there, Abs. I'm gonna have to do it again."

"Was Joan there?" Abby asked, still trying to process and get all the information. Aaron shook his head.

"No, she wasn't there. Or I don't think so anyways. Halee was the youngest, there were about a dozen."

"Aaron, I know this sucks, but you had no choice. You know Max wouldn't have wanted you to break our cover yet. He'd want us to keep looking for Joan."

Aaron nodded miserably. They had all agreed prior to coming in that the priority would always be the girls. They were to be saved at all costs, even if that meant leaving others behind. It had been an easy choice to make when they were all safe planning this, but now that the possible reality was upon them…

"No wonder they let us in with infected in tow. They're collecting them! This is fucked."

Aaron nodded again in agreement and for several minutes, they both sat in silence.

* * *

Oblivious to what was going on with the others, Tara was surprised to find herself enjoying Cam's company. Though she had intended to use him, she was surprised to find he was actually a really nice guy. He reminded Tara of Joshua, her boyfriend who died during the initial outbreak. They chatted through their entire shift, and Cam invited her back to his quarters for dinner. When she asked about it, he told her he'd been there long enough to have a small space of his own.

Stepping into his bunk, Tara was surprised at the neatness and personal touches. He had converted his room into what resembled a tiny apartment, complete with faded floral sheets and a small hotplate. A few old pictures lined the wall.

"Nice sheets," she teased, sitting on the edge of his bed as she played with a piece of the worn fabric.

"Target was sold out of the skull and crossbones," he joked sitting beside her. "I have a surprise for you."

"Oh yeah, what's that?" she smiled.

"Close your eyes."

Tara obliged him and squeezed her eyes shut until he declared she could open them. When she opened them, it was to a glass jar filled with reddish liquid.

"Is that…"

"Yup! Spaghetti sauce!"

Tara squealed in excitement. Though their community had many things, tomato seeds were one they rarely had, and earlier in the day, she and Cam had been talking about favorite foods from pre-FIRE. Tara's was spaghetti.

"Oh my gosh, where'd you get that! That isn't 8 years old, is it?" she asked with a hand on her hip as she eyed the jar suspiciously. Cam laughed.

"Of course not. I grew it. Well, I grew the tomatoes anyway. One of the nurses who stays onsite at the compound waters them when I have to leave; we split the crop fifty-fifty."

The two of them settled into preparing their simple dinner. Tara knew she would have to meet up with Abby and Aaron soon and figure out their next step, but for now this small slice of normality was something she intended to enjoy.

Chapter 23

Clara huffed with exertion as she took down their tent. Everything was sopping wet after a night of rain, and she was miserable. As if not knowing what was happening with Max and Joan wasn't enough, it had to rain too. Their makeshift tents weren't meant to withstand long term, much less British Columbia rain, and everyone else was in similarly poor spirits.

Finally finished, she told Seventeen she was going to go for a short walk. She needed to move or she was going to go crazy. Walking the opposite direction of the base, Clara took a deep breath and took in the smells of the wet forest, so similar to home. The earthy smell of damp wood and dirt mixed with the fresh smell of water from the stream she walked beside.

Home, she thought, *home is Max and Joan.* Not for the first time, she wondered what they would do when this was finished. So distracted in her thoughts, she didn't hear a voice calling out to her from ahead.

"Clara!" A voice cried again, finally breaking her from her thoughts. Looking up, her mouth hung open as she saw who was coming towards her.

"Sam!" Clara exclaimed. Sam paused in front of her, chest heaving. Wiping the wet hair from her face, Clara paled as she took in Sam's worried expression.

"Why are you here? What happened?"

"More," Sam replied, still trying to catch her breath. She had been running almost non-stop, and had made it to the base in just over a day. "More people coming."

Clara led Sam back to the others, doing her best to remain calm despite her body vibrating with tension.

"Sam?" Bear said as they walked into their camp. "What are you…"

"Everyone come here!" Clara called out, interrupting Bear. "You need to hear this."

Once everyone had gathered around, Sam spoke quickly.

"Brian and Sarah came back," she said. "There are a bunch more non-infected, at least fifty but probably more. I don't know what's happening, but there are a lot and they are armed and they are coming this way. They said in the south a few communities have been totally ransacked. Guy has people posted at home, but they seem to think they are coming to the compound."

Everyone began talking amongst themselves until Lake predictably piped up.

"Quiet down, quiet down." After a moment, the group stopped to listen. "I knew this would happen. We have to go back and keep our people safe, there is nothing we can do for the others now."

Clara stepped forward, outraged, but before she could say anything Tonya walked up and slapped Lake, a resounding and loud noise. The look on his face would have made Clara laugh if not for the situation.

"You assholes," Tonya declared, "my daughter is in there! Clara's daughter! Our people! Coward." She spit at his feet before turning to the rest. "I'm not leaving until I have my daughter back, or I'll die trying."

Clara stepped forward. "Me neither."

Much to the two women's dismay, much of the group decided to go with Lake, leaving only Sam, Tonya, Seventeen, Clara, and Bear remaining. Clara was surprised Sam was staying, but she explained she left Griffin with a friend of hers, Angela. He had a bit of a crush on Angela's daughter, Ava, and was happy to stay with them. For now, Sam's place was here. Everyone, except of course Lake, did express their apologies; they couldn't take on another fifty or more uninfected. The rain had dampened everyone's spirits, and after not hearing from anyone inside in several days they all doubted they would.

The remaining four watched as the rest walked away.

"So," Tonya said, turning back to them, "what the hell do we do now?"

Chapter 24

Max stared at the door with longing. Vague impressions and ideas fluttered through his mind, but he couldn't make sense of them. His brain was processing things at a crawl, and he had yet to solve the riddle of the doorknob. On the other side of this door he somehow knew was freedom and...something else. The feeling of forgetfulness was increasingly unnerving, though he couldn't have put it in those words, or in fact any words. He felt trapped in his own mind, unable to express the emotions he was feeling. He also felt as though he should be able to speak, but when he opened his mouth nothing but a low moan came out. Shaking his head, he continued to try to focus.

That morning a man had come to take him and someone else away. The man covered in markings and metal seemed vaguely familiar too, but Max's thought process stopped there. They stared at each other for a while but couldn't communicate, and didn't even know how to try. They were led to a large room, easily the size of a small warehouse, lined with cage after cage. Though he should have felt surprise, Max didn't notice or care about the dozens of other infected in the cages. Without struggle, he was brought into one and the door shut behind them.

A new door.

Max refocused his efforts as much as he was able, a small line of drool dripping from his mouth. Around him, a hundred other infected did the same.

Chapter 25

Michele finished the final preparations for her first major procedure with Joan: a brain biopsy. The girl hadn't taken to Michele's latest speech very positively, acting odd and withdrawn afterwards. Michele had let one of the soldiers take her back to her room, wanting to give the girl time to process. She hoped that having the night to think about it would redirect and remind Joan of their previous conversations, of how she could help humanity. Michele did not bargain for the strong-willed child though.

One of the nurses rushed into Michele's office. "Problems with the girl, come now," was all she said before turning and rushing back down the hall.

Michele entered the room to see Joan was snarling and growling at the guard trying to take her from her cage. Having been instructed not to hurt the girl, the young soldier looked at Michele with confusion, obviously unsure of how to handle this.

"I dunno what to do!" he exclaimed. "She ain't never been like this before!"

"Joan!" Michele cried, stepping up to the cage. "What's gotten into you!?"

Joan growled at Michele, "You can't use me!"

Michele looked at the girl with shock on her face. She knew the girl had seemed off yesterday, but this was beyond what she expected.

"Joan, I..."

Snarling once more, Joan turned to face the wall, putting her back to Michele, who stood there dumbfounded. *Maybe separating the other girl from Joan wasn't the right idea...* As much as she wished she could take the time to calm the girl and regain her trust, she had to get this done. It would certainly be easier if she were cooperating, though. Their supplies were limited, and it was all ready to go. It couldn't wait. Sighing, Michele turned to the soldier.

"Everything is already set up. Do what you need to but please try not to hurt her."

With a heavy heart, Michele left to get herself ready for the biopsy.

* * *

Joan thrashed against the gurney that held her, both fury and sadness filling her. Michele left the room and the soldier had essentially tackled her, strapping her to this awful thing. Joan could lift her head slightly, but otherwise was totally immobilized. Tears covered her face at the realization that this would likely be her life from now on. Her parents would never find her and she would be here, forever an experiment for the uninfected.

It seemed to take forever to get wherever the soldier was taking her, and she paid little attention to their surroundings until they entered one room and an unpleasant smell filled her senses. It was the smell of many unwashed bodies with an undercurrent of rotten food. Though there were no shouts, a dull but persistent noise filled the air. Groans, moans and the breathing of a lot of people. Lifting her head, Joan's eyes widened as she took in the rows and rows of cages of people who looked like her, like her parents. She prayed they weren't putting her in with them, until she remembered Halee and began scanning the cages to see if her friend was okay.

There are so many of them!

From her vantage, she couldn't see very well but didn't see anyone small enough to be her friend. Just as she came to the end of the row, she caught sight of a familiar face.

"DAD!" she shouted, watching her father's face. He was here the whole time! He did come for her! He had gotten her mother out of this place once before, he could do it again. Hope filled Joan, but slowly deflated as they passed. Max didn't raise his eyes or acknowledge Joan's voice. No recognition came, and with a heavy sadness Joan slipped by, watching her father's blank face stare at the door in front of him. Passing through the second set of doors, they left the room of infected behind. She was wheeled into a stark silver and white room then left alone, still strapped to the gurney.

* * *

Michele sat in her office with her head in her hands, considering the news she was just given. Joan was secured and in the surgery, but that wasn't what was bothering her. Well, that wasn't totally true. It did bother her that they had to resort to force to secure her. Since Joan had been with them, Michele had truly grown to like the inquisitive and bright girl. Doubt about what they were doing had been creeping into her mind for days, and what she was just told only reinforced that.

"Michele?"

She turned to see Nikki standing in the doorway and gave her a wan smile.

"What's going on?" Nikki asked, taking a seat next to her.

Michele sighed and rubbed her face. "It's Joan."

Nikki shrugged, "I know she isn't taking it well now, but she'll get used to it. To us."

"No, no it isn't that."

"Then what?"

"I—Private Terns took her to surgery, she's there now." Nikki nodded, indicating Michele should continue. "Joan, she apparently cried out 'dad' on their way through room C. He didn't know if she actually saw someone because of how packed in they are." She raised her head and met Nikki's eyes. "Nikki, I can't do this."

Nikki frowned at her. "What do you mean you can't do this? Because the kid saw someone she thought was her dad?"

Pushing her chair back, Michele began pacing.

"My sister wanted to help the infected," Michele began, ringing her hands together as she walked. "This doesn't feel like helping, Nikki. I keep thinking 'what would Rachel do?' and you know, I don't think this is it. I think she would have let Joan go. How can I keep her here?"

She looked up at Nikki but couldn't decipher the infected woman's expression.

"We'll never find a vaccine if we let the girl go," Nikki replied bluntly. "It's one girl for the good of the world. Michele, we can't let her go."

Sighing, Michele nodded. She knew this. But even still, she couldn't help but ask herself the same question on repeat. *What would Rachel have done?* But Michele knew the answer to this, because Rachel had done it. She had let an infected, pregnant woman out knowing she could be the key to something more.

I've got to get Joan out.

* * *

Aaron walked with the appearance of calmness, making his way down the corridor towards the med station. He had been instructed to find a doctor named Michele, one of the head researchers working within the facility. After speaking with Abby, they both agreed that, for now, he had to keep up the facade, even if that meant having to do another dose of the serum. In the meantime, he would be able to get a better idea of the base layout and the number of infected within. Abby was getting a feel for the guard schedule and shift changes, so when the time came, they hoped to sneak everyone out without being noticed. Neither had seen Tara since the morning before, but assumed that she was doing her part as well.

Walking into the med bay, Aaron found it almost empty except for one woman with curly blonde hair, her back towards him. She seemed to be alternating between an old-school microscope and madly scribbling notes. Aaron cleared his throat to get her attention.

"Ahem, hello. I'm Aaron. I was told you would be expecting me?"

The woman scribbled one more note before turning around. "Hello Aaron, yes, thank you for coming. I'm Michele." Standing, she walked over to shake his hand.

"I understand you are quite new here but have some medical and military background?"

"Yes ma'am. I've been helping Private Yards with the serum doses; he said there might be something else you needed help with?"

"Yes, actually. We'll be needing several more specimens for a round of testing. All of our subjects have been dosed so there shouldn't be any risk, but since there are so many in such a small space I prefer someone competent to assist with retrieving them. I also need help with transporting one who isn't subdued, but I don't anticipate she'll be any trouble for you."

Aaron nodded. "That isn't a problem. A dozen subdued infected should be easy enough to get through, even if one isn't dosed."

Michele let out a small laugh.

"A dozen? Wherever did you get that number?" Aaron looked at her, frowning. He knew at least Joan was kept elsewhere, but hadn't gotten any indication of more than that.

"The cage," he replied slowly. "We brought a couple new ones with us, but there couldn't have been more than about a dozen in there?"

Michele gave him a small smirk. "Come with me."

Just as they were about to exit, an infected woman walked in. Aaron recognized her from his first day in Captain Cords office.

"Hey Nikki," Michele greeted, "I'll be back in a few minutes. I just need to show Aaron to room C and get Joan back."

Nikki nodded and continued over to her work station. Michele led Aaron out at a swift pace.

"Who's Joan?" Aaron asked after a moment, trying to be nonchalant about the question.

Michele seemed to hesitate before answering. "A young infected. She…we need her for some of our work. Dosing her would affect my tests, which is one of the reasons I want your help."

Aaron nodded but didn't ask any further questions, not wanting to arouse suspicion. They walked for several minutes before walking into a large room. Aaron stopped at the door to take in the sight of what was before him. Dozens and dozens of infected, at least a hundred of them but probably more, in cages lining the walls. The lighting was incredibly dim, and he guessed they had little care about illumination for what they considered zombies. There were probably ten or fifteen per cage, but they all seemed so tame. Docile. Dosed.

Swallowing deeply, he followed Michele, who barely glanced at the infected.

"These have all been dosed and aren't used regularly," she explained. "The cage B you went to is for the ones that have the capacity to assist in some way as well as for newer acquisitions. Slowly, but surely, we will rehabilitate them all, but for now this is the best we can do to keep them calm and contained. This way, please."

As they got closer to the end of the row Aaron recognized Max and Kenny among some of the others. Max was staring intently at the door to the cage, unmoving. Keeping his eyes straight ahead, Aaron kept going. At least he knew where the infected were being kept now.

They walked out a second set of doors and down another hallway until they got to what looked to be a surgery room ahead. A frown crossed Michele's face as they looked ahead and saw a number of people, including Captain Cords, in the room already. They were surrounding a young infected girl who was strapped to a gurney, a stark bandage wrapped around her head. Michele burst into the room with Aaron only a step behind.

"What's going on here?" she asked immediately. Aaron hung back, waiting to see how this played out while sneaking glances at the young girl who he assumed to be Joan. She did very much look like a younger version of her mother, though she had her father's curly dark hair. She appeared to be unconscious but other than the one bandage, seemed unharmed.

"Ahh, Michele," Cords said turning to greet them. "Good of you to join us."

"Why are you here, Stephen?"

Cords eyes flashed with anger as he reached out and backhanded Michele, causing her to cry out and hit the floor. Aaron tensed but didn't move.

"That's Captain Cords, Doctor Samborski," Cords said, kneeling beside her. "You think I'm stupid, huh? You think I don't know about everything that goes on around here?"

"W-what are you talking about?" Michele responded, her cheek now an angry red.

Cords stood and laughed, brushing invisible lint off his pants. "You really think I would allow zombies to reproduce? More zombies in the world?

And did you think I would let you release the one zombie that could actually save us? You are out of your goddamn mind, doctor." Cords motioned to the soldiers behind him. "Take her to room C. Nikki will be taking over the doctor's work. Dr. Samborski is no longer fit for her position." He turned to leave, ignoring the cries and shuffles behind him as the soldiers took Michele. Cords stopped in front of Aaron, sizing him up.

"You," Cords said to him, causing Aaron to stand at attention, "you know where room B is?"

Aaron nodded in affirmation, not trusting his voice to speak.

"Take the small one there. Nikki will be taking over, you may take your leave when you are done and report to Nikki tomorrow."

<h1 style="text-align:center">Chapter 26</h1>

Michele kept her head high as she was led through the cold warehouse room and into the cage at the end of the row. About ten infected were standing around, barely even flinching as the creaky door was opened. Only one seemed to be watching, but it quickly turned its attention back to the door. *Thank god the serum helps with the aggression-smell issue*, she thought as the door closed behind her. The last thing she needed right now was to be attacked by infected.

Going to the back of the cage, she sat down against the wall and stared ahead. This was not where she expected to be right now, and she needed to figure out what to do next. Cords had said Nikki was taking over, and since she hadn't spoken of her concerns to anyone but Nikki. She could only assume that it was she who told Cords. Michele wondered why Nikki would have done this, but it was irrelevant now. She needed to focus on what she could affect from here.

Outside the cage she watched as the new recruit, Aaron, wheeled Joan through the doors. Before he passed Michele jumped up and ran over to the edge of the cage.

"Aaron," she whispered loudly to attract his attention. He paused a moment, looking around to ensure no one but them and the zombies were in the room before walking over to her.

"I can't help you," he said quickly. "What do you want?"

Michele nodded. "I understand. Can you do me a favor though?"

Aaron eyed her a moment. "No promises. What is it? I gotta go."

"Private Terns told me Joan had called out to one of the zombies in here earlier. Can you try to find out who it was?" Michele watched Aaron's eyes widen slightly, darting over to the infected man who was staring at the door with intensity.

"I'll be back," Aaron whispered before turning and taking the unconscious girl down the hall and away. Sighing, Michele went and took her place back against the wall.

Michele must have fallen asleep because the next thing she knew, she was awoken by a voice loudly whispering her name.

"Michele, wake up," the voice said.

Groaning, she pulled herself up off the cold concrete and made her way back over to the cage door where Aaron was standing, furtively looking between both ends of the row for anyone coming through.

"Sorry, I couldn't come back until I knew I wouldn't be missed."

"It's okay, thank you for coming back period. What time is it?"

"Late," he replied. "I came back because you were asking about the girl. Why do you care?"

Michele stared at him for a moment. She felt as though she were being tested, and wondered if this was another trick. *Well, I'm already in here. What have I got to lose?*

"I've been working with the girl for a while now, whose name is Joan, by the way. She is unique, and we believe she may hold the key to a cure or vaccine. I heard she had called out to someone in these cages, thinking her father was in here. I told a colleague that I felt badly keeping Joan here and wanted to let her go. Obviously, Cords found out and didn't like that, so now I'm here," Michele answered honestly. "Why do *you* care?" she questioned him.

Aaron watched her for a moment before nodding approvingly. "Okay," he said as he pointed at the infected who had been staring at the door earlier, who was now asleep along with most of the others. "That guy right there, his name is Max. He is Joan's father. We both came here to try to rescue her, but to keep my cover I had to give him the serum almost two days ago."

Michele listened with wide eyes. "Incredible! Are there any more of you?"

Aaron stared at her but said nothing. Michele coughed lightly. "Fair enough. What can I do to help?"

Aaron considered this. "Do you know how they re-dose the serum with the ones in here?" he asked. Michele nodded.

"Yes, they put it into the water and food. Too much time to inject or give it individually to each one. I can try to keep him from drinking, they only feed them once every five days or so because of their metabolism. It would still likely be a day or two before he came back to himself, but it varies. Some take longer, some don't recover at all. Plus, I have no idea if they intend to keep me here or feed me at all. I may very well be useless myself soon if I don't get some water at least."

Aaron thought about this a moment. "I'll try to get you some water but I'm not sure when." He then pointed at another infected, a tall man with tattoos and piercings covering much of his skin. "Him too, please. Take care of them."

"Okay. How are you going to get them out though? And I trust you can appreciate that if I'm going to do this, I expect to go with you when you leave."

"I don't know the plan exactly yet. But yes, if you can do your part to stay ready and watch my friends there, I will do what I can to let you out when the time comes. I have to go, but I'll be back when I can."

Michele watched the young man exit back through the doors before taking up her place at the back of the cage again, keeping an eye on the two infected Aaron had pointed out. How she was going to keep them from eating or drinking, she didn't know, but she would certainly try.

For Joan.

She watched the infected man; Max, Aaron had called him. Something about that name rang a bell to her but she wasn't quite sure what it was. It wasn't as though Max was a terribly uncommon name. Sighing, she did her best to get comfortable and go back to sleep. It wasn't until she was on the cusp of consciousness that she remembered where she had heard that name. Michele immediately sat upright and looked over at the man again, who was asleep a few feet away. *Rachel's notes! That is what the pregnant zombie said her husband's name was!*

Although this realization didn't help her much right now, she at least knew she was right about Joan. She was that same zombie's daughter, back here somehow after all these years. *If this is her father,* Michelle thought, *where is the mother?*

Chapter 27

Joan groaned loudly as she began to regain consciousness, her body cold and stiff against a concrete floor. Was she back in her cage? The last thing she remembered was being strapped to that table and being poked with something. Cold seldom bothered Joan, but she would never forget the feeling of ice being pushed into her body. Then there was nothing.

She brought her hand up to her head and felt some kind of fabric wrapped around it. Her mind still felt fuzzy and confused and she had to shut her eyes as soon as she opened them, the bright lights too much. As her vision finally cleared, she realized she was no longer alone, but neither was she in the room she had seen her father in. Swallowing deeply, she looked at the faces surrounding her. Joan quickly recognized the infected man who brought her food before, standing around among several others. None of the others in this new cage were familiar, until one of them stepped aside revealing a young girl who had been hidden among the adult infected.

"Halee!" Joan cried out, jumping up as fast as she could to go over to her friend. Halee didn't respond at all and continued to stand there.

"Halee?" Joan said again, grabbing her friend by the shoulders and forcing Halee's face towards hers. She looked deeply into her eyes and saw no remnant of the vibrant girl she had befriended. A sob escaped from Joan's lips and she let her hands drop. Just like her father had been, it was like Halee wasn't herself anymore. Joan looked at the others around them, noting immediately that they all had that same vacant expression. A tear fell from Joan's eye as she watched them. Is this what Michele had meant by a cure? Is this what they would do to her too?

Unsure of what else to do, she took Halee by the hand and brought her to the back of the cage. With minimal prompting, Halee sat down beside her. Joan kept their hands clasped together, waiting for whatever would come next.

Unlike her previous room, she had no pillow, no blankets, or any other small comforts. Just a large cage filled with infected and a couple buckets in the corner. Joan finally fell asleep with Halee beside her, the soft snores of the other infected the only sound in the room.

Joan was deep asleep when a whispered voice brought her back to the edge of wakefulness. She blinked a few times, her brain taking a moment to catch up with her.

"Cam?"

"Sssh," he replied. "Come here for a sec."

Joan untangled herself from Halee, laying her friend gently on the floor before making her way to over to Cam.

"What do you want?" Joan spat. Although devastated when she was first brought here, the hours she had spent unable to sleep had grown a deep anger at what had been done to her. Done to her dad, to Halee. Cam had helped her before, been somewhat nice to her even, but so had Michele, and look where that had gotten her.

"I wanted to make sure you were okay," he replied with a sad look on his face. "I know you don't trust me, I don't blame you. I just wanted to see if you were okay."

"I-I," Joan opened her mouth to respond but only a small choked sound came out before she started bawling. Cam threaded his fingers through the cage in front of her, saying nothing. "Cam, what did they do to these people? They're like mindless…"

"Zombies," he finished for her, not looking particularly happy about it. "I know, Joan. That's the idea."

Joan's teared ceased as she glared at him. "They are people, not zombies!" Cam stepped back, raising his hands in surrender.

"I know, girl, I know. Listen, I can't stay, but hang in there, okay?"

"Why did you come here?" she asked again.

"Let's just say I met someone who changed my mind about people like you." With that, he left.

Joan sat in the same spot, staring at the door he had exited through. While she didn't really understand, she finally made her way back over to Halee, where she curled up again and cried herself back to sleep.

* * *

"Hey," Cam said as he walked into Abby's bunk where she and Tara were sitting. "I saw Joan."

Earlier that day, Tara came to Abby to implore her to include Cam in their plans. The two of them had gotten close over the last few days, and Tara was confident he was sympathetic to their cause. He had even spoken about Joan a bit, having to bring her here and how the others had been so cruel to what he considered just a little girl. Unable to find Aaron to talk it through with him, Abby made the decision and reluctantly agreed to speak to Cam. Tara had good instincts and Abby was inclined to trust her friend's judgement. Plus, if she was being honest with herself, they needed the help.

The three spent the evening talking. Abby questioned him intensely before finally telling him why they were at the compound. Luckily, Tara had been right, and Cam immediately agreed to help. He told them he hadn't been happy in this place for a long time, but in the world of FIRE, being alone wasn't an option. Cam also told them that now that he was being given a different option, especially one with a beautiful woman, he absolutely wanted to help. Tara of course giggled at this; Abby rolled her eyes.

When Aaron finally made his way back and told them all that had transpired, Cam quickly agreed to go check on the girl, while Aaron went to check back on Michele, Max, and Kenny. They agreed Aaron was to use his best judgement to decide what, if anything, to tell Michele. Based on what he had overheard, they all agreed it was likely she would be sympathetic to their cause as well as a great asset.

"And? How was she?" Abby asked impatiently, wanting to trust the soldier but still uneasy in his presence.

154

"She is pretty upset but seemed unharmed and was willing to talk to me, for a minute anyways. I checked and she had a brain biopsy done earlier so she has a bandage around her head, but otherwise she's fine," Cam replied, sliding in beside Tara and clasping her hand.

Abby nodded and was about to open her mouth when there was another knock at the door. Aaron entered, quickly shutting it behind him.

"The doctor will help," he quickly told them, "but we need to make sure to get them some water that isn't tainted. Cam, will they feed her or anything, do you think?"

Cam considered this a moment. "I'm not sure," he told them honestly. "Most of the time defectors are killed or let loose. But she knows a lot, and from what you said I think she pissed Cords off something fierce. I've never seen them put a human in with the zombies."

"They are all human," Abby snapped quickly, causing Cam's face to redden. "I didn't..."

Tara stilled him with a hand. "He didn't mean it like that, Abs," she defended. "Give him a break, okay?"

Abby sighed and brought a hand to her head to squeeze the bridge of her nose. She was feeling defensive and jumpy and didn't like the new odds stacked against them. How would they get everyone out, especially with everyone so spread over the compound?

"You're right, sorry Cam."

He shook his head. "No apology needed. You're right, I've just been here so long I'm so used to thinking of them like that, even though I know it isn't right."

"So, now what?" Aaron asked, changing the subject.

Everyone looked at each other, shaking their heads.

"Well," Abby finally said, "we should try to connect with everyone outside or send them a message somehow. Cam, you know how this place works best. Any ideas?"

"Patrols haven't been going out like normal," Cam replied. "Something is going on, but I don't know what."

"Can you try to find out? Maybe try to get outside and find Clara and tell her what is going on?" Abby asked him.

Cam nodded. "Yeah, I can do that."

"What do you want me to do?" Aaron asked her.

"You just worry about Max and Kenny for now. See if you can get them all some water or something. How long did you say until that serum wears off?"

"Can't say for sure, the doctor said it could be a day or a week or even not at all."

Abby nodded. "Well, either way we'll get them out, but it'll be a lot harder if they don't know what's going on. So that's your job. Tara, you work with Cam and try to find out what is going on and why things aren't running like normal around here. People like you, so try to make some more friends and see if you can find anything out."

"Aye, aye," Tara replied with a mock salute. "And what about you?"

"I'm going to try to focus on Joan and how we can get her out. See if I can get her to trust me at least, so when the time comes, she'll go with us without a fuss."

"Good idea," Cam told her, "but she doesn't trust uninfected very much, so you'll have your work cut out for you."

Abby nodded. "Okay guys, we need to get a move on this. Every day seems to bring a new set of problems. We meet back here tomorrow night, okay?"

Everyone agreed and made their way back to their own beds. After they left, Abby sat in her bunk and considered their situation.

We have seven people inside now, if we include the doctor and Cam. We have no way to get Joan or the others out of their cages. We have no way to get out of the base without being seen, much less through the guard watch. We have no idea what is going on outside. Both Max and Kenny have no idea who they are.

Over and over, she looped their many problems over in her head, unable to come up with solutions for any of them. Eventually, she fell into a fitful sleep.

Chapter 28

Captain Cords sat over his desk, considering his own next moves. He was expecting the Birmingham recruits to be here any day and had hoped to make a bit more headway on the vaccine. Cords knew of some of the raids on zombie bases in what was once the United States, and though he wouldn't consider himself a zombie advocate by any stretch, he still aimed to avoid mass extermination. Hence him allowing Michele to work as she had for the last few years. He certainly hadn't been expecting his top researcher to betray them and wondered how much this would hold them back.

Grumbling, he opened his drawer and pulled out a lovely bottle of aged Whiskey he had liberated and kept for himself. There were only a few shots left in the bottle, but after today he felt he deserved a drink. He poured a glass and took a sip, sighing deeply in contentment as someone knocked on the door.

"Come in," he responded, after putting his glass out of sight. He wasn't about to share the nice stuff with the damn recruits.

Nikki sauntered into the room, closing and locking the door behind her.

"Nikki," he said gruffly, taking his glass back into his hand.

"Hello, Captain," she replied with a smile, walking around his desk. Cords returned the smile as she straddled his lap, taking off his hat and putting it on her own head.

"What do you think?" she asked teasingly. "Would I make a good Captain?"

Cords chuckled and took another sip of his whiskey before putting it down and wrapping his arms around her. She immediately leaned down and kissed him deeply, which he returned willingly.

"Mmm, missed you," Nikki whispered as she stroked his face.

If you had asked Captain Stephen Cords a few years ago if he could ever be attracted to a zombie, he would have laughed. The thought was so abhorrent to most that it was a bit of a joke even among the soldiers. Cords had heard more than one joke about "zombie dick" and what would happen if a zombie got hungry while you were "in the middle." Cords had always been proper, though. By the books and a man of his word, and a man for the people.

Two years ago, though, he had a late night after having to let one of his men go. It was never an easy thing for him, and that night was the only time since the FIRE virus struck that Cords had let himself get drunk. He had been sitting in his office, lamenting, when Nikki came in. Her dark chestnut hair flowed against her pale skin and for the first time, he saw her as a woman. Since then, they had been meeting in secret. It was the only time in his life he had ever really, truly broken the rules. Well, that and the hundreds of subsequent liaisons. Thankfully, the test Nikki had developed after she turned proved that Cords was immune to the virus.

An hour later, they were lying in his bed wrapped in sheets. He knew he would have to make Nikki leave soon; it was his one rule that they could never let the others find out. So in tune with him, though, she was already getting up and beginning to dress as this thought crossed his mind.

"Are you ready to take over the research department?" he asked her, sitting on his elbow, admiring her firm naked body as she dressed. She turned and gave him a wicked smile.

"Oh, ye of little faith!" she mocked. "Of course I am."

He grunted softly in response. "The new recruits will be here in a few days. When can you start?"

"Really, Stephen? You are all work and no play. We can talk about this in the morning, can't we?"

"No rest for the wicked," he replied.

She gave him a wry look as she pulled her shirt back on.

"Give me two days," she told him. "I need to prepare the team for a full dissection, make sure we have the storage ready and everything in place." Nikki planted one last kiss on his head before turning towards the door.

"And you're sure we shouldn't keep the girl? This is the best way?"

"Stephen, baby. Have I ever steered you wrong?"

Chapter 29

Michele was sore, hungry, and thirsty by morning. She groaned when she woke up on the cold hard floor and it took a moment to orient herself before she remembered what happened the day before. Grumbling, she pushed herself up off the ground, noting the other infected were already up around her, still just standing around. Michele looked around, taking note of Max and the other infected man, and grateful to see that no one had brought water yet. She didn't think feeding day was for another few days, so at least she only needed to keep them from drinking. If she could make it that long herself. She tried to swallow, but already her mouth and throat felt dry and parched. Not having anything else to do, she made her way over to where Max was standing.

"Max?" she tried first, watching for any reaction.

Nothing.

Gently grabbing him by the hand, she led him to the back of the cage and sat next to him. He put up no resistance but said nothing and never took his eyes off the door.

"Max," Michele began again in a loud whisper, "I know you don't remember anything, but I'm Michele. I know your daughter, Joan. I never met her, but my sister knew your wife, Clara. Do you remember Joan and Clara?" She watched him closely, noting how his brow scrunched together ever so slightly. *The names,* she thought.

"Your daughter, Joan, is very pretty," she continued. "I bet she gets those good looks from her mom, Clara. Am I right?"

Max turned his head slightly, as though listening. Encouraged, Michele opened her mouth to continue when the doors to the warehouse pushed open.

"Any zombie thiirssttty?" a voice rang out loudly, followed by a laugh. Michele frowned, leaning over to see who was entering. She wasn't surprised to see Private Yards, who was frequently assigned to various zombie duties, and was pleasantly surprised to see Aaron behind him.

"So, just put the water in the cage?" she heard Aaron ask.

"Yeah, just put one container in the bucket and put one in each cage. These fuckers are still pretty dumb, but they've figured out how to drink from their hands at least."

"Okay," she heard Aaron reply. "I'll start down at that end."

Michele watched as Aaron made his way down the long hall, starting at the cage across from her. She watched as he dumped in a canister of the serum and put a bucket into the cage. He turned, making his way over to the one she occupied. She said nothing, of course, but saw him go through the motions, pretending to pour the already empty canister into the bucket. Her eyes lit up but quickly dimmed. This solved some of her problems; after all, she could at least not die of thirst now and didn't have to worry about keeping Max or the other from drinking. Her eyes wandered around the other occupants of the cage and she swallowed deeply. She knew those two, at least, wouldn't harm her when they regained their memories. But the others… Well, it would be interesting to see if any of those in here with her were of the more aggressive variety.

She caught Aaron's eye, but he quickly looked away. Sighing, she got up with the others and went over to grab a drink, grimacing at the state of the bucket. Hopefully he had a plan. Otherwise she may very well end up zombie chow before she could get out of here.

A few hours later, the bucket was empty and the infected were once again standing around when Michele decided to keep trying with Max. He had a mild response to hearing his wife and daughter's names, so she would keep using that.

For the rest of the day, Michele stood beside Max just talking to him. Asking questions she didn't expect him to answer, and saying "Joan" and

"Clara" as many times as she possibly could. By evening, Max was indeed watching her, but still had said nothing.

* * *

Clara and those who stayed behind made a pitiful picture. The rain had finally stopped the night before, but the entire area was covered in mud. They were all miserable and felt like they would be permanently wet. Though the infected didn't feel cold as much, it didn't make their current situation any more pleasant.

"Do you think the rain is keeping the others?" Tonya asked for the hundredth time. Clara sighed. She understood the other woman's desire to see some action but was at a loss for what they could do. They hadn't seen a sign of anyone in the days since the others left and knew that a lot more uninfected would be here soon. Clara simply didn't know what to do.

"Maybe," Sam replied for her.

Moaning, Clara stood up.

"This is ridiculous," Tonya declared. "We've got to do something!"

"But what?" Sam asked.

They had had this conversation several times over the last few days but hadn't been able to come up with anything.

"I have an idea," Bear said, surprising them all. The three women looked over to him, making him flush from the attention.

"We can't go inside or do anything like that," he began, ignoring how Sam rolled her eyes at the obvious statement, "but if you guys, I mean, if you ladies are right and the rain is stoppin' those reinforcements, maybe we can hold them up even more."

"What do you have in mind?" Clara asked curiously. Anything was better than sitting around.

After a short discussion, Tonya and Seventeen stayed behind to keep watch while the other three left into the forest to see how they could stall, or stop, the impending soldiers.

* * *

Tonya sat on a mossy boulder, looking down at the expansive base while Seventeen was scouting the surrounding area. Every fiber of her being wanted to go down there, demand they give her daughter back. It took everything she had to just sit there and wait. At least now she was doing something though, even if that something was nothing. A bell tolled below, and she saw the familiar pattern of the guard change begin, something that happened three times a day.

She watched with disinterest as the current people went inside, and a new group came out. It wasn't until she counted them when she realized there was one more than usual. Frowning, she pulled out the binoculars to look closer and saw that a blonde man was being let out of the compound gates. Her eyes widened in fear. What if he found Seventeen or the others? She quickly rushed to gather their few things together and hide them in a hollowed out log they had chosen for exactly this. With practiced stealth, she made her way down the embankment to see what the man was doing, hoping Seventeen would also see him and hide.

* * *

Cam had a productive morning and was thrilled that he was able to complete some of the tasks Abby had assigned to him. He'd had issues with what they had been doing for years, and still found it hard to believe that a pretty red-headed girl had come and changed it all.

That morning, he had already discovered another group of recruits from Birmingham were on their way and managed to make an excuse to go outside to collect some more plants they used regularly for the serum. Cam hadn't told Tara or the others yet, but he was an integral part of the creation of the serum and it was something he was now deeply ashamed of.

In his previous life, he had dabbled in horticulture and knew many uses of different plants and herbs. It was because of this Cords had assigned him off base so often. He had been able to identify and bring back all sorts of things they used for both medicine and food. A few years before, he had come across a certain type of datura plant that he knew was not only used as a hallucinogen but also for sedation and other things. Originally, he had been trying to make a kind of anesthetic, something less volatile and easier to make than ether, but that isn't what he ended up with. Using a mix of hyoscine and other plants, he created a kind of serum that didn't knock people out as intended. Instead, it acted almost like scopolamine to the infected, making them incredibly docile and suggestable. Once Cords found out about it, he ordered testing on zombies and they quickly discovered that it made them infinitely more manageable.

Some of the infected who took the serum maintained enough intelligence to be able to do small jobs around the base, and the rest just stood silently, not causing problems.

Even though this wasn't its intended use when he started working on the project, it saddened him to think that, intent or not, it was because of him the serum existed. For the most part, he was able to put it out of his mind. Their life at the base, and outside of it, left little idle time.

Meeting Tara had changed so much for him though, and brought back a flood of emotions and memories he long thought suppressed. He snorted as this thought occurred to him. Sounded like what he had heard of zombie memory returning. Maybe later he would tell Tara that she was his FIRE and see what happened. He grinned when he thought of how gorgeous she would look with those freckled cheeks all red and flushed.

Shaking his head and returning his focus, Cam stopped to assess his surroundings. Now wasn't the time for these thoughts; he needed to find the people who were, presumably, hiding in these hills.

Once he reached the top of the slope and got out of sight from those guarding the base below, he slowed his pace. He had on him his usual weaponry, the bow and arrow as well as several knives. Wanting to ensure anyone in the area didn't see him as a threat, but not willing to give them up completely, he put the bow over his shoulder and kept his hands face-out at his sides. There was still a risk that a mindless infected could be in the area, but they were rare nowadays this far out. They all knew of small bands of aggressive ones roaming the country, but so far they hadn't seen any signs of this close to their home. Plus, he was confident he could take one or two on, even hand to hand. Scanning the area, he noted how dense the forest was up here and slowed himself further.

Most of the valley below was covered in the base, dotted areas and buildings around one central hub, all surrounded by the ugliest fences in history. Though they served their purpose, it was a mish-mash of random materials put together to supplement the fencing that surrounded it originally. Rolling up the hills, though, was just green. Miles and miles of forest with one road in and out. A road that now was cracked and broken, the years allowing nature to reclaim what was hers. Not that the road was necessary. Cars had been mostly obsolete for years, gone with the expiry of gasoline and diesel. They had a few electric cars on base, but they weren't used and were only intended for emergencies. Like life rafts if the worst should ever happen. But it hadn't, and the cars sat mostly unused.

It was a strange time to be alive in the world with FIRE gone, but at the same time not gone. While the infected did outnumber the immune and uninfected, the smarter infected had banded together separate from them. An uneasy sort of truce had been in place for years, but with what was happening further south, they all knew that wouldn't be the case for long.

Cam sometimes thought about what would happen if all the infected banded together. There were a decent number of smart ones, and if they truly wanted to, he was sure they could wipe them out.

But they hadn't.

Most of what he had heard through the grapevine over the years indicated that they avoided confrontation. Just like the uninfected did, before recently.

A twig snapped ahead, and he immediately stopped, remembering to keep his hands outwards and raised.

"I'm not here to hurt you," he said. After a moment, a woman stepped out from behind a tree. She was quite small but looked to be in her forties. Her skin was alabaster and her eyes pale just like the rest of her kind, but a very human and angry expression covering her face immediately betrayed her intelligence. That, plus her pointing a bow and arrow right at his head.

"Don't come any closer," she warned, stopping maybe ten feet from him. If he wanted, he could get beside her in two big steps and she wouldn't even have time to shoot

"I won't, I came here to find someone. Abby and Tara sent me to find Clara." The woman's eyes twitched. "I'm trying to help. Are you Clara?" The woman stared at him for another moment before lowering the bow slightly. At least it was pointed at his feet now.

"No," she said shortly. "Why are you here? Why haven't you called your friends down there? Or taken me down with one of those knives on your belt? I know you could."

Cam did his best not to smile. "You're right, ma'am, I could, but I won't. My name is Cameron, or Cam. Like I said, I am friends with Tara and Abby, which is why I haven't called anyone and why I won't. They couldn't come out, but I could. So here I am." Once again, the woman studied him, as though trying to figure out if he was lying. Her eyes darted around for a moment like she was looking for someone. After a minute she deflated, fully standing down.

"Okay, Cameron. I'm Tonya. I don't know if I believe you, but I'm kinda bored right now. So why don't you put down your weapons there, and we can go over this way and so you can tell me a story."

This time, Cam did smile. "Okay, Tonya. I can do that."

Chapter 30

Michele did her best to get comfortable and ignore the cold of the warehouse. Throughout the day she had tried to move around a bit, cozying up to Max as much as was acceptable while she talked and did her best to stimulate his memory. She didn't know much about the other infected that Aaron had told her to take care of, but also managed to get him sitting closer so she could talk to the two of them throughout the day.

She thought back to the only turning she had been present for: Nikki's. It had been a hard time for their people, with Nikki being the first scientist exposed. For years they had been so careful, had so many failsafes, and it was merely a fluke that resulted in Nikki's infection. It all happened so quickly after Michele arrived, but since it was one of her first assignments, helping with the memory stimulation stuck with her.

It had taken months for Nikki to truly get back to a level that was close to where she was before, but within days she had begun to talk and recognize the people around her. Michele knew that the serum acted in a different way than the virus, though. Their experiments with the serum had shown a range of recovery from hours to weeks and even a select few who never seemed to return. Michele could only hope Max and his friend were on the shorter recovery end. She thought about this, and what tomorrow would bring, as she finally drifted off to sleep.

* * *

"Max, stop it! Joan'll be back any second," Clara said, the giggles betraying her true

feelings. Max merely wrapped his arms around her tighter, nuzzling into her neck.

"I bet I can find something for her to do for a while," he whispered into her neck, eliciting more giggles. Max loved that sound.

"Mommy, daddy!" A voice called out from behind them, causing Max to groan. Clara pushed him away, kissing his cheek.

"We're over here, baby," Clara called back just as Joan burst through the trees.

"Come see, come see!" Joan cried with excitement as she hopped from foot to foot, only barely waiting for her parents to start moving before dashing off again.

Max gave Clara a small smile, despite his disappointment, and grabbed her hand to follow their daughter.

As they approached the north side of the island and got closer to the shore the wind picked up, the trees dancing in the cold autumn breeze.

Joan stopped a little way from the water, waiting until Max and Clara came up behind her.

"What are they?" Joan whispered, wonderment in her voice. Max stopped to pick up their toddler, hugging her close before answering.

"They're seals," he answered, keeping his voice quiet. "They don't always come here, so it is very special that you found them."

"Wow," the small girl whispered. "They are so big, dada!"

"They're beautiful, aren't they?" Clara commented, bringing her hand up to brush down Joan's hair. Max looked over to his wife and daughter and his heart swelled. They spent the rest of the afternoon watching the majestic creatures until they finally slipped back in the water.

It was Clara who finally broke them from their moment, standing and holding out both her hands for them.

"Come on, let's go home."

* * *

Max woke up gasping. It took him a moment for him to get his bearings but the cold floor beneath him and the sounds of dozens of bodies breathing around him brought him back to reality quickly.

"Joan," he whispered, finally remembering where he was, "Clara."

Moving over to lean against the side of the cage, he squeezed his eyes shut to try to remember everything. His brain felt slow and foggy, not unlike when he had first woken up after FIRE. Max recalled Aaron coming to see them, injected him and Kenny with something….

Max quickly looked around and found Kenny lying a few feet away, a blonde woman next to him who was clearly not infected. He frowned for a moment trying to recall who she was but came up blank. Reaching over, he shook Kenny's shoulder until the man woke up, turning to growl at whatever had woken him.

On seeing Max's face, the man relaxed slightly and only watched Max for a moment before lying his head back down.

"Kenny, wait," Max said before he could fall back asleep. "You've got to remember. It's me, Max."

This time, Kenny sat up still confused, but with a hint of recognition in his eyes.

"That's right, man, it's me. You've got to remember."

"Max?" a feminine voice said from behind him. Max turned around to see the blonde woman awake and watching him.

"How do you know my name?" he asked warily. The woman sat up and Max could tell she was suppressing a groan. If the floor was cold and uncomfortable for his infected body, he imagined it was much more so for her weaker, uninfected one.

"We met yesterday," she told him as she got up, "I'm the one who made sure you didn't have any more of that serum. Even still, I'm amazed you're talking already."

"Serum? What are you talking about? Who are you?"

The woman shifted forward and held out her hand. It took Max a moment to connect the gesture, but when he did, he shook it.

"I'm Michele. I work here, or did anyways," she frowned. "Your friend, Aaron, came and told me about you. He had no choice but to give you the serum, a special formula created in the compound here to revert infected back to their non-memory state, minus the aggression. You have to keep taking it though, so when Aaron saw me here, he asked me to keep you and your friend there from taking any."

Max looked over at Kenny and then back to Michele. His head still hurt, and he was having trouble making sense of things, plus naturally being suspicious of non-infected didn't help. But how would this woman know of Aaron, or his name, if she wasn't telling the truth? Closing his eyes, he tried to concentrate, opening them to see Michele looking back at him.

"I also know your daughter," she said in a quieter voice. Max jumped forward, grasping her arm.

"Joan? Where is she?" he asked, panicked. Michele's eyes got wide as she hissed lightly in pain, making Max realize how tight he had grabbed her. Releasing her arm, he moved back slightly.

"Is she okay?"

Michele rubbed her arm and nodded slowly. "I think so," she replied, "but I don't know for how long."

* * *

"Little Joan," a voice called out, "wake up."

Joan groaned as she sat up rubbing her eyes. She looked over to see Nikki kneeling beside the cage watching her. Joan frowned.

"What do you want?" she asked insolently as she wrapped her arm around Halee, who was still asleep curled up beside her. Nikki let off a small laugh.

"Oh sweetheart, why the anger? I never did anything to you," Nikki responded sweetly. Joan just glared at her.

"You let them do this to Halee," Joan spat at her. "You're no better than Michele or any of the other people in this place." At hearing her words, Nikki's facade dropped, and she stood staring down at her.

"Well, it's too bad that you don't want to be my friend. I could have made your last day much more pleasant," Nikki said matter-of-factly before turning to leave. Joan jumped up, grabbing the cage.

"What do you mean last day? They're letting me go?"

Nikki laughed, this time with a much more sinister cadence, and walked out without answering Joan's question.

"Nikki!" Joan yelled after her. "What are they going to do to me? Nikki!" But the woman was already gone. Joan let go of the cage, dropping to her knees.

I have to get out on my own.

Joan sat there for several minutes looking around the room before her eyes fell to the one thing that would release her. The door. With determination she stood and made her way over, reaching her small hands through the bars. It was locked with a simple key and Joan's mind went back to a book her mother had read her once. It was a mystery story and in it, the heroine had been locked in a room and needed to use a bobby-pin to get free. Joan wondered if that would actually work.

With renewed vigor, she made her way around the room to poke at each of the infected in the room. A few grumbled at her as she looked through their hair and pockets, but most stayed asleep and ignored her. When she got to the last one she still hadn't found a bobby pin and frowned, trying to think of what else she could use. Her eyes landed on one infected who was wearing a worn leather belt. The shiny buckle caught her attention and she smiled to herself.

Joan rushed over and pulled the belt free, the infected putting no resistance. Holding it to her face she inspected the frame and prong.

I can do it....

* * *

Nikki walked down the hall towards room C with a pep in her step. After all her planning and patience, she was so close to finally having a vaccine in her grasp. To finally curing herself from the nightmare that was being an infected.

Practically dancing, she entered the large warehouse, wrinkling her nose at the smell that permeated the room. Slowing her steps, but keeping the smile on her face, she approached the end cage and laughed out loud at the sight of a filthy Michele sitting at the back of the cage.

"How are your new friends treating you?" Nikki asked, still laughing.

Michele said nothing, just glared back at her.

"What, nothing to say now? I'm hurt, I thought we were friends," Nikki said with a mock sadness in her voice. Michele's eyes flared.

"What kind of friend gives up another? After all I've done for you? After all we've done together, all we've accomplished, why?"

Nikki's laughter and mirth quickly heated and turned to anger. Her lips thinned into a line as she looked at Michele with disgust.

"What kind of friend would give up another one's chance at a normal fucking life?" Nikki spat back. "Zombie babies was bad enough, like more fucking infected is a good idea, but then you had to go and say you were going to let the little bitch kid out. You knew we needed a fucking autopsy to get a real cure, you knew how bad I needed it, wanted it. But that didn't matter, because some fucking kid missed her daddy." Nikki started to turn. "You being here? This is on you, *Samborski*. Tomorrow, I'm getting my fucking cure."

With that, she turned and exited the room.

* * *

Max watched and waited as the awful zombie woman left the room. It took everything in him not to reach through the bars and throttle the woman, but he knew now wasn't the time for hasty decisions. Joan had less than a day. He felt a hand clasp his shoulder and turned his head slightly to see Kenny standing there.

"How long will it take?" Max asked him. Michele watched them quizzically as Kenny walked over to the lock and inspected it. Max had spent the entire night with Kenny talking to him and was rewarded close to dawn with Kenny's recognition. He was also rewarded with a short laugh when Kenny went on a long, curse-filled tirade on what had happened.

"Not that long," Kenny told him. "They never took my tools, but this is a bit higher tech than I'm used to, plus my head still feels a bit off. Still, a few minutes? Five at most." Max nodded.

"So, this whole time you could have escaped?" Michele asked them incredulously. "Why didn't you?" Max continued his pacing, leaving him to answer the woman.

"We needed to make sure we could all get out and save Joan. We came in this way, stealthy, on purpose. Breaking out right away would have negated that completely, and if we were recaptured or killed, it would have put suspicion on the others who brought us here."

Michele nodded in understanding.

"Okay, so you can pick the locks. Then what? There is still a base full of people to get through. And even if you can do that and get Joan, there are still guards outside. All the time."

Max turned and looked at her, a mix of anger and frustration on his face. He knew she was right. They had no real plan. But time was against them and they didn't have any other option. They had to get out. Tonight. He growled and slammed his hand against the gated cage, making several of the occupants jump. Max looked around at the rest. They hadn't been fed the serum either. Even in the other cages, Max noticed that many of the infected watched when he spoke. Michele told him that was part of how the serum should work, making them highly suggestable. She speculated that they would be particularly so to their own kind.

"Kenny, do you know anyone else in here?" Max asked him as he studied the other occupants. Kenny glanced around the room. The other infected he knew, Bill, had been left in the other room, but he pointed at one dark haired woman who was watching Max with glazed eyes.

"Her," Kenny told him. "I don't remember her name, but she was one of the slower ones they took from the compound months ago." Max nodded and walked up to the woman, lowering himself to her eye level and taking her cheeks in his hands.

"Can you understand me?" Max asked, staring into her eyes. The woman blinked, frowning slightly. Michele and Kenny both watched with interest.

Max sighed and let go of her face, still staring at her. After a moment, he walked to the opposite end of the cage and turned to look at her again. She was still watching him. Max pointed at her, then beckoned her over.

"Come here," he instructed, still waving her over to him. The woman frowned again but took a tentative step forward. And then another. Until she was standing beside Max, who had a smile on his face.

"They can follow at least," Max stated, and Kenny smiled in understanding.

"And?" Michele asked, obviously not understanding the implications.

"How many cages in here?" Max asked her, ignoring her question as he tried to count from his vantage point.

"Twelve," Michele answered. "Just over a hundred infected between them all, if I'm not mistaken."

"So, how long do you think it would take you to open them all?"

Kenny hesitated a moment. "Once I get the hang of these locks it would go pretty quick. Maybe thirty or forty minutes for all of them." Max nodded before turning to Michele.

"Do you know how often they come through here? In particular at night?"

"Not often, I don't think," Michele admitted, "but I'm not positive. There haven't been issues for so long that I doubt they put much man-power into watching this room though. We haven't had enough energy for video surveillance in a long time."

Max paced the small area for a few more minutes, finally stopping and resting his eyes on a woman on the other side of the gated cage beside him. With purpose he strode up, curling his hands around the cage and staring intently at the infected woman.

"Can you understand me?" he began simply, watching her for a reaction. Her glazed eyes stayed fixed in the distance, but that didn't deter him.

"Listen!" he said, louder this time. The woman slowly raised her head, looking in Max's direction, but said nothing. There seemed to be no comprehension in that blank stare, but Max knew all too well by now how that slow recognition worked. When he was sure he had her attention, he continued talking to her. Not really saying much of anything, just talking. Michele and Kenny just watched.

* * *

It was late into the night when Abby was finally able to sneak down to see them. Max had managed to grab the attention of many of the infected in the adjacent cages, but none had spoken, only listened. Michele chattered away about how interesting it was the serum allowed that much focus, but Max paid little attention. When the door to the warehouse opened and he saw Abby's small frame poke through, he breathed a sigh of relief in seeing her.

"Fuck, guys! You're, well, awake!" she exclaimed. Max gave her a small smile.

"Thanks to Aaron, and Michele here. I'm glad you're here," he told her, shifting gears. There wasn't much time to tell her what his plan was.

Chapter 31

It took Joan several hours but she finally managed to remove the prong from the belt and use it to unlock the door. Standing in the now opened cage, she looked over at Halee and realized she had another problem. She wasn't big enough to carry the older girl, but she couldn't leave her here. She also needed to find her dad somehow and get out of the compound without being seen.

This is hopeless! No. I can do this. I just need to find someone to help.

Joan looked back at Halee once more before nodding to herself. Yes. She would go get help then come back for Halee. Letting a small smile cross her face, she turned to open the door just as Denny walked in. His eyes shot open in surprise but his expression quickly changed to a sinister grin. "Going somewhere, little zombie?"

* * *

A few hours later, the infected were released. Many stayed within their cages, still unaware they had been freed. Max and Kenny spent a lot of time wandering the masses, speaking to them long enough to grab their attention. By the time they were through, all eyes were on them and Max looked at his people with pride. Serum or not, he would lead them out of this place.

"She'll sound the bell any time now," Kenny said to no one in particular. Michele hung back biting her finger nails with worry. She had heard of the devastation left behind when Rachel had released infected years before. And that was only a fraction of how many they had now.

"Max," Michele said as she approached him, "you can't let them kill everyone." Max's face hardened at her words. While he was no monster, it was this base, these people, that had kidnapped and held both his wife and daughter now. Mercy wasn't high on his list of cares at the moment. Michele seemed to read this in his face.

"I know you owe these people no favors, but many of them had nothing to do with Joan's capture. If you can forgive me for what I've done, then I implore you…I know you can't stop them all, but please, do what you can to make sure this isn't a massacre?"

Max sighed and gave Michele a wry look. "You know you're a bit of a pain, right?" Michele gave him a small smile back. "Kenny, come here a sec."

He made his way over to Max, with a few infected following him. They stopped inches behind him.

"Back off a bit guys," Kenny told the infected before turning back to Max. "They certainly like us, anyways. What's up? Is it time? I thought we wanted to wait for the bell?"

"We do," Max told him, "but I have a different plan for you. I need you to lead these people out and meet me by the front. Don't kill anyone you don't have to, let's keep casualties to a minimum. We're better than these people."

Kenny frowned a bit but nodded, "What about you?"

"I'm going to save my daughter."

When the bell rang overhead for a shift change, they moved.

Kenny shouted and cajoled most of the infected to follow him right away, with only a handful staying behind still watching Max intently. The two men gave each other one final meaningful look before Kenny raced down the hallway. Max looked at Michele.

"Where would Joan be?"

Michele paled, seeming to consider what the day would bring for the small child if they didn't do something.

"Probably surgery prep," Michele admitted as she swallowed deeply.

"Let's go."

* * *

Clara stood at the top of the hill and watched through the binoculars as the confused guards began to make their way back inside. She had gotten pretty used to the shift change bells and knew this one wasn't at the normal time. The shift was almost over, but not quite. The guards seemed to know it too but were trained well enough to listen.

Clara, Sam, and Bear were successful in finding the non-infected the day prior; however, they hadn't been able to stall them without revealing themselves. They would be arriving at the compound within a few hours at most. Sam and Bear stood beside her, their hands together, and Tonya paced the forest behind while Seventeen tried to keep her calm.

"What's taking them so long?" the woman cursed, only to be shushed by Seventeen.

"They'll get them out," Seventeen reassured her. "Just be ready."

* * *

They raced through the halls towards the surgery, Max pushing his body as fast as it would allow. The first infected woman he had spoken to followed him closely, a few others a bit further behind them.

"Which way!?" he shouted as they hit a fork, no longer concerned with stealth. Everything in his body was screaming for his daughter, telling him to move.

"Left," Michele answered quickly as they darted down the hallway. "Door at the end."

Max rushed down the last of the hallway and burst into the room, frantic to save his daughter. He entered to see Nikki and several other non-infected dressed in scrubs. *Joan.* He almost choked as he saw his daughter laid out on the steel table. He couldn't see any blood, only a white bandage around her head, but her eyes were closed and she was strapped down on her limbs and forehead.

Max roared as he leapt towards the first uninfected coming at him. Without losing momentum he slammed his fist into the man's face, effectively stunning him with a single punch. Another came up behind Max, but before he could turn the infected woman from the cage dove on him. The man screamed as she tore at his face before leeching onto his neck. Blood poured out of the bite wound, but Max didn't stop, leaving the woman to her prize.

Nikki stood on the opposite side of the table, holding a scalpel in her hand which was pressed up against Joan's throat.

"Back the fuck away from my daughter," Max growled at her, trying to assess how he could get the sharp object away from his daughter's neck.

Nikki glared at him, "Daughter, huh?" and pressed the scalpel down just a fraction, a small line of red spilling from the cut. "Huh, guess that's why she tried to escape."

"Nikki!" Michele cried from behind him. "You have to stop!"

"Betraying your own kind, eh Samborski?" Nikki mocked, not removing the scalpel. Michele narrowed her eyes.

"You're one to talk."

Nikki only smiled at this.

Max rushed around the table, not willing to wait another moment. Nikki panicked at the sudden motion, stepping away from Joan. She reached out to slash at Max, slicing across his chest. He dove at her, heedless of the blood now pouring from his wound, wrapping his hands around her small neck. Max's face was twisted in fury as he tightened his grip, causing Nikki to drop the scalpel.

"Max, no!" Michele cried. "She's not worth it. Come help me with Joan."

Max glowered at the woman a moment longer, giving one final squeeze which eliciting a satisfactory final squeak from Nikki. He released his grasp and Nikki tumbled to the ground as she gasped for breath, holding onto her neck which was already turning red and blue.

Once Max confirmed she was down, he rushed up to the table, picking up the scalpel to cut Joan's bonds. Her tiny wrists tied down made him want to sob and he had to keep his hand from shaking as he released her first hand. Behind him, he felt rather than saw Nikki move and before he could turn around Michele jumped passed him, engaging the enraged zombie. Max watched as Michele held Nikki's arms, keeping the needle in the woman's hand away from her own body. He could see that Michele was beginning to get Nikki's arm down, overpowering her, when some kind of realization crossed Nikki's face. With a smile, she dropped the needle, causing Michele to falter slightly, before Nikki reached forward, tearing her teeth into Michele's arm. Michele shrieked as she pulled back, bringing her bitten, bloodied arm to her body. Nikki stood back with a grin, blood dripping from her face onto her white coat.

Max watched the two women circle each other as he finished cutting the last of Joan's bonds.

"Guess they'll be your kind too now," Nikki said with a smirk. Just as Max finished and was about to come to her aid, Michele growled as she grabbed another scalpel and with a burst of speed she rushed forward, slicing it across Nikki's neck. Pure shock crossed Nikki's face, as though she couldn't believe what had just happened. Her hands came up to her neck, trying fruitlessly to stem the flow now pouring from her neck. She made a gurgling noise as she dropped to her knees, finally falling face down into a pool of blood.

Max reached over for Michele, who whipped around to look at him with a frantic look in her eyes.

"I-I'm not immune," Michele sobbed, her eyes wide with fear. Max held her arm, which wasn't bleeding too severely, and looked into her eyes.

"You will always have a place with me. I will take care of you. But first, I need your help."

Michele swayed where she stood and, for a moment, Max was worried she was about to drop. After a second, she seemed to compose herself, nodding at Max.

"Let me wrap this up, and we can get Joan out. We have to leave."

Chapter 32

Abby and Aaron rushed down the halls and into the madness. They had just sounded the shift change bell. They knew once the outside guards got inside and saw the infected had been let loose the replacement shift wouldn't be going out, leaving the entrance unguarded.

Assuming the other uninfected didn't arrive in the meantime, that is. Before they could worry about that, they needed the rest of their team.

"Where is the surgery? And where the fuck is Tara?" Abby said behind her as they jogged down the hall.

"That…" Before Aaron could finish, they saw Michele and Max round the corner in front of them, with Joan passed out over her father's shoulder.

"Max!" Abby cried out as they all stopped in the corridor. Abby looked down at the unconscious child for a moment then up at Max, giving him the smallest of smiles before her face fell back to serious once more. "Have you seen Tara?"

Max shook his head. "No, where would she be?"

"I don't know," Abby said with dismay. "I can't leave without her."

Max frowned. He knew that the girls had history together but wanted to get Joan out as quickly as he could. He debated with himself for a moment, but Abby and Tara had done so much for them. Abby was right, they couldn't leave without her.

"Alright, let's go. Aaron, where did they keep Joan?"

* * *

Cam and Tara bolted through the hallways towards room B. The guard bell meant they didn't have much time, but they were both determined not to leave anyone behind. Bursting into the room, one guard, a mountain of a man, stood there with a look of shock on his face at their abrupt entrance.

"What the hell…" Before the man could finish his sentence, Cam hurled a knife with deadly accuracy, pinning the man in the center of his chest. A few gurgles could be heard before the man dropped. Tara looked at Cam with utter shock and not a bit of judgement.

"Trust me, he was an asshole," Cam told her. "His name was Denny and I guarantee if you knew him, you would have done the same."

Tara nodded, not questioning it further before rushing over to the cage. It wasn't huge, holding maybe ten infected, several of which were lying in a pile sleeping. She quickly scanned but didn't see any sign of Joan.

"Can you open this?" She asked Cam, not taking her eyes from inside the cage. As he went over to the dead man to grab his keys, one of the infected in front of Tara moved, revealing another small form.

"Halee!" Tara cried, looping her fingers into the mesh of the cage. The girl didn't move at her name being called but several in the pile began to wake up from the loud noise. "Hurry, Cam!"

A moment later, the cage opened, and Tara rushed in, heedless of the others or any danger that might be present. She knew and lived with so many infected that there was no fear for her. Cam watched her and Tara noted the look of worry in his eyes as well as something else. Guilt perhaps? Tara didn't know what that look meant, but knew it wasn't the time to find out. She knelt down, holding Halee's chin in her hand.

"Halee?" A blank stare watched her, causing Tara to sigh.

None of the infected seemed to realize it was open or make any move towards the door.

"Come on, help me with her," Tara said to Cam. "If the others follow then great, but we need to get moving."

Fortunately, it took very little cajoling to get the girl to follow them. Tara's eyes filled with sadness as she watched the once bright and vibrant young girl follow so absently.

They moved through the corridors and towards the front entrance as quickly as they could with the slow-moving girl, a few infected trailing behind. Tara could only hope they would find their friends there. Stopping close to the mess hall, Tara peered around the corner, noting that there were several soldiers awake and wandering around.

"What do we do? There's no other way to get outside, is there?" she asked in a whisper, turning to Cam. He shook his head before peering around the corner himself. He knew all the people that were there, including Jake, the ultimate asshole. He had seen that man torture people on a whim, including pitting vicious infected against his own kind, and various other atrocities.

"Lead Halee over here, I can take care of them." Tara paled a bit but nodded, leading the younger girl around the corner. He heard her whisper instructions to stay put as he began to pull out his blades. Before rounding the corner, he handed Tara a machete from his belt.

"Just in case," he told her, not pausing to see if she had more to say before stepping out into the hallway.

"What're you doing here with all this shit going on?" Jake immediately growled out at him. Merritt and Clark immediately stepped out from the room behind him. Cam said nothing, gripping the hidden knives harder in his hands. Jake laughed and it took Cam a moment to realize why before he caught the flash of a few of the other infected from the cage following behind him.

"Walking the zombies?" Jake mocked before nudging his head in Cam's direction. Clark and Merritt immediately grinned and pulled out their own weapons, Merritt favoring her bow staff, while Clark was more of an edged weapon guy, like himself.

Merritt shouted as she rushed towards him. Cam put one foot back, bracing himself as he raised his twenty-inch needle point blade to meet her staff. As soon as it hit, the vibrations carried up his arm, almost making him drop the knife. With no time to hesitate, he brought up his other hand, driving the hunting knife up to her gut. Hot blood poured over his hands as the infected behind him came to action. They dove on the woman, barely allowing Cam the few seconds he needed to scramble away. Clark let out a scream as he jumped at Cam, almost gutting him and only missing by inches. He heard Tara cry out behind him but couldn't spare the time to see if she was okay as he grappled with Clark. Though they were similarly built, Clark had years of experience on him, not to mention a calculating ruthlessness that Cam lacked.

Out of the corner of his eye, Cam saw a few more infected rising from the dead woman's body to go after Jake, who was watching this all happen with an amused look on his face. Anger burned in Cam's mind, giving him the added strength to push Clark forward, making the man trip over Merritt's now very dead body. Before the man could rise, Halee jumped out and tore her teeth into the man, making him cry out. Cam watched in astonishment as the tiny zombie ripped out his throat, blood pouring over her.

"Cam!" Tara cried out in warning as Cam cried out, a sharp pain reaching across his back. Stumbling back, he turned to see Jake with his own knife in hand, grinning like a maniac. He had quickly taken the two infected out who attacked him. They now lay dismembered in the hallway. Letting out a growl, Cam tackled Jake in the middle, surprising the man. Both their weapons were lost in the melee as they rolled, each trying to get the upper hand. Cam was quickly getting overpowered by the stronger and more ferocious man.

"You killed my fucking team," Jake spat out through gritted teeth as he finally brought his hands up to Cam's neck. Cam immediately felt his airflow cut off and his face begin to darken. Just as his vision began to fade, he caught a flash of orange hair and movement above Jake and immediately felt the hot spray of blood pour onto his face. Jake fell forward dead and Cam pushed the heavy weight off of himself.

He looked up at Tara as she stood; he stopped for a second to admire her. Though her face was flushed, her multitude of freckles seemed to dance against her skin, her eyes bright and alert. A few splatters of blood mingled in and her mouth hung open slightly, breathing deeply as she held the bloody machete in her hands. He had never seen anything so beautiful.

Scrambling up, he gave her a charming smile, kissing her quickly, but deeply, before grasping her hand and pushing forward. Halee quickly followed.

* * *

Max darted down another hall upon hearing screams of pain, almost crashing into Tara, Cam, and Halee, who came around the corner at the same time. He stopped for a moment and took in the three of them, all soaked in blood and heaving.

"Are there any more?" he quickly asked.

Tara shook her head. "No. There were a few more infected but we didn't have the time to get them to follow."

Abby came around the corner, crying out in happiness as she rushed forward to hug Tara. "Are you okay?"

"Yeah, I'm fine. Where's Kenny?"

"He's got the rest of the infected with him, he'll meet us by the front."

With everyone accounted for, they ran towards the front doors.

* * *

Stephen Cords stomped through the compound, making his way towards the surgery rooms. The moment he heard the shift change bell go off early he knew something was wrong; his internal clock was too well set on the base's schedule despite how close the timing was. The halls seemed quieter than usual, and deep in his bones Cords knew it was something to do with that damn kid.

He told Nikki it was a bad idea to go ahead with the dissection so quickly with so many other things happening. He had a new group arriving from Fort Dearborn any day now and still had his misgivings about killing a child. Even a zombie child, and even for a cure.

As Cords turned the last corner before the surgery he paused, seeing a few drops of blood down the hallway. Cursing, he rushed down the last of the corridor, pushing open the doors to the surgery.

The room was in shambles. Scalpels and other implements he didn't know the name for littered the ground and there was blood everywhere, not to mention the body of one of the nurses, whose name he didn't know. It was obvious that an infected had gotten at her by the bites visible on her arms and face. He couldn't see the child anywhere.

Cords brought a hand up to his face, rubbing harshly before going around the table. He froze as he caught sight of another body.

"Nikki!" he cried, as he rushed over to her body. Heedless of the blood he lifted her head to his lap to reveal the deep gash across her neck. Her pale eyes, dead and unseeing as they looked up at him.

He took a few deep breaths, closing his eyes as he said a silent prayer. When he opened them, his eyes caught sight of a paper sticking from Nikki's front pocket. Cords reached down, opening the paper and his eyes widened as he read what was on it.

No wonder Nikki had been so intent on getting a cure quickly, he thought. *She was pregnant.* Leaning down to kiss her head one last time, he gently put her body back on the ground before putting the paper into his own pocket.

Chapter 33

Max strode out the heavy doors of the compound with Joan over his shoulder, immediately taking a deep breath of fresh air. The morning light was crisp and bright to his eyes after days of being indoors.

They found Kenny close to the entrance, doing his best to hold back the hoard of semi-aware infected, though a few had obviously gotten out before them, judging by the half dozen bloodied corpses in the vicinity. The rest came into the courtyard behind him, many of them shielding their eyes from the bright natural light. Max's moment of triumph was short-lived, though. He stopped and looked out at the gate in front of them. Abby had done a great job in ringing the shift change bell and inside the gates there were no living soldiers remaining. The other soldiers had all gone inside to take care of those problems after hearing the bell ring. On the other side of the gate, however, were dozens of armed uninfected, and they were staring straight at them. Reinforcements had arrived.

Max turned to look at those following him. They had managed to get this far, and he had no intention of losing any of their people now if he could help it. Aaron walked up to him, keeping his eyes forward.

"Give me Joan," he said and Max darted a glance at him.

"No, I've got her." Max replied, squeezing Joan closer to him. Aaron turned to face him.

"Let us help," Aaron said, "trust me. I'll make sure she's okay."

Max looked down at his daughter, reluctant to let her go. Raising his eyes he looked around at the infected, and uninfected, surrounding him, watching him and waiting for his next move. Taking a deep breath, Max handed Joan over to the man.

To help Joan, truly save her, he needed to learn to trust. And to save their people, he needed two hands.

* * *

Clara watched as Max and Joan stepped out the doors and panicked at the sight of her unmoving daughter, a bandage wrapped around her head. When she looked at Max's face however, she saw no heavy grief and knew she must just be unconscious or asleep. Her relief didn't last long as she watched her husband hand Joan to Aaron and step forward into the courtyard.

A moment later, a large group of infected poured out into the courtyard behind him. The few remaining guards were previously disposed of, but Max stood now looking towards the compound gates and the new mass of people standing between them and freedom. Gripping the log in front of her with ferocity, she waited to see what each side would do next.

* * *

Max looked over the rows and rows of uninfected on the opposite side of the gates, all with fury and outrage written on their faces at seeing the group of zombies converging at the front doors. *What bad timing,* Max thought wryly. If they fought their way out, they could likely win with the numbers on their side, but at a huge loss of life on both sides. As he considered their options, a voice rang out behind him.

"You're trapped, you may as well surrender."

Turning around, Max saw Captain Cords step out with a group of soldiers behind him. While there were still more infected than not, he wasn't wrong. Max could see Kenny and the others were having trouble containing the infected from pushing forward, now that they saw their captors at their back. Growls and roars ripped among the crowd, a barely contained frenzy. Even the serum couldn't hold back this level of fury now that the smell of blood was in the air.

"Max," Abby whispered coming up beside him, her eyes wide, "what do you want us to do?" Max looked down at the girl's brown skin and then beside her at the pale faces of the infected. He turned back to Cords.

"You will lose a lot of your own people too," Max stated simply but loudly enough for everyone to hear.

"You already killed the person who mattered most," Cords growled at him. "So, you *are* one of the smart ones." His eyes darted to Abby, Cam and Tara. "I knew something was off with you folks." Then his eyes landed on Michele and they widened slightly, taking in the red bandage on her arm and the pallor to her skin, then Joan in Aaron's arms.

At this moment, a handful of infected broke free and rushed towards the soldiers around Cords. Screams rang out over the courtyard, punctuated by howls and moans. The infected managed to take down several soldiers but were quickly taken out by the remaining. Max cringed at the efficiency with which they killed his people.

"Keep them back!" Max shouted to Kenny and the others, who were struggling even more to contain them. Max knew this couldn't last much longer and turned back to Cords.

"We just want our people," Max said loudly. "We won't hurt anyone, we just want to be free and to live in peace!"

Many of the soldiers, both in and outside the gate, laughed at this declaration. Weapons were raised, with even a few guns in the mix, a rarity, while both groups of uninfected waited for their orders.

"Cords," Michele said, stepping forward, "you know the numbers as well as I do. We can't sustain further loss of life."

Cords stared at Michele, seeming to consider this statement, making Max's measure of the man increase. Unlike the previous Captain, whose throat had been ripped out by Max himself, he felt this one wasn't simply here to kill zombies, like it seemed so many of the uninfected were. He considered Cord's comment about having killed the person he cared most for already and wondered who it had been.

"Captain, let us in!" voices shouted from the other side of the gate, the soldiers eager to come in and fight. Max kept his attention focused on Cords.

He knew this man would make or break them. Minutes passed and even with the shouts and moans from both sides, Max felt the stillness of the moment. He sensed the moment of decision in Cords but wasn't sure which way that decision leaned. Just as Cords went to open his mouth, a loud banging rang out behind them and Max heard the gates crash open.

The other soldiers were through.

* * *

Bear watched as Max spoke to the uninfected man at the compound doors, Sam's hand gripped tightly in his own. Though he couldn't hear what was being said, he guessed Max was pleading their case, and it didn't look like successfully. He looked down at the masses of people in the valley below. So many infected, his people. So many uninfected pushing to get into the compound. Rage and anger evident on so many faces.

It was strange to think that only a few short weeks ago, he was roaming the country with Squid and Steve. Even stranger to think that they had been a part of capturing some of the infected below. The rewards that seemed worthy at the time now made Bear feel ashamed at his own greed and self-interest. A small pang of guilt struck him as he realized how little thought he had given to his two friends' deaths, but he knew it had all happened for a reason. Bear had never been religious, but since meeting little Joan he knew his life had changed. Since meeting Max and Joan, he had a purpose. Squeezing Sam's hand, he waited and watched.

His eyes drifted down to the uninfected at the gates, widening as he realized one of the men below held wire cutters in his hand. The people behind him stopped pushing, giving him the room to cut the gate open. A cry of anguish let out of Clara's throat and he watched as the gates opened and the uninfected poured in.

Turning to Sam, he saw tears shimmering in her eyes as she gave him a small nod. He gave her a grateful smile before letting out a loud war cry and darting down the hill towards their friends.

* * *

Aaron spun around as the gates behind them crashed open. Still holding Joan in his arms, he looked around catching sight of Tara standing there holding Halee's hand; the little girl still looked quite absent.

He rushed over to them and looked into Tara's face. "I know you can fight, but right now you need to protect. Can you take the girls?" Tara paled, looking at the incoming uninfected before nodding, taking Joan into her own arms. Despite how young she was, Aaron could see Tara struggled to carry her, being such a small woman herself. He pointed to an alcove on the side of the building.

"Take the girls over there. Michele, go with them. Cam, take care of them." He didn't wait to see the other man's nod of approval before turning and rushing into the fray.

* * *

Max watched as Aaron rushed over to Tara, getting the young girls out of the way. The soldier who was with Tara stood in front of them, weapons raised.

Trust. I need to trust.

Seeing that Tara and her partner were watching after his daughter, he turned his attention back to Cords, who paused only briefly from his frantic shouts at the new arrivals.

"I never wanted this," Max said as he looked Cords in the eyes.

With a mighty roar, Max turned and rushed towards the incoming soldiers. The first who approached paused at the look of absolute madness Max knew was written across his face. Without stopping he pulled out the scalpel he still had and tore it across the man's throat, not pausing when the blade stayed stuck. Abandoning his weapon, he turned to face the rest. One man ran towards him and Max growled before ducking, taking the man out from the middle. Diving on him he pounded his fists into the soldier's face. Blood coated his fists and he only stopped when the man ceased moving. Behind him someone else tackled him off the man, raising a huge club above his head. Before Max could react, the man was lifted off his chest and tossed into a nearby group. Max looked up into a familiar scruffy face. Bear reached his hand down, helping Max up.

The men looked at each other for a moment before taking in the scene around them. Never had Max smelled so much blood. Screams punctuated the air, now in pain and not only anger, as well as a couple gunshots. Max watched as one soldier raised his gun and fired, only to have it backfire and blow off his own face.

Despite the serum, the infected obviously had no problems with attacking with the proper motivation. Screams on both sides filled the air, the sounds of thuds and blades hitting flesh still loud and clear. A cacophony of chaos and death. Piles of bodies were already spread across the compound, blood shining against the pale skin of their peers.

No. This wasn't what Max had wanted at all.

* * *

Abby met the oncoming soldiers with coordinated fury born of years of practice. Growing up, her father had taught her how to handle guns plus other weapons and over the years since FIRE, she had perfected many of her skills. Despite her stature, she was a force to be reckoned with and didn't hesitate to defend herself, and kill, if necessary.

The first soldier she met seemed to falter for a moment, she assumed because she obviously wasn't infected. Taking advantage of his hesitation, she brought up her machete and slashed without mercy. A shout at her back turned her around but before she could raise her weapon once more, an arrow struck her prospective attacker through the chest. She looked over to see Aaron, giving him a quick nod of thanks before turning back into the chaos.

Doing her best not to think of who she was killing, Abby gritted her teeth and swung her weapon, heedless of the tears that were streaking down her face.

* * *

Max looked over at his daughter to see Tara and the other man standing in front of Michele, Joan, and Halee, weapons raised against a group of uninfected approaching. Bear caught sight of where they were looking and both men ran to their aid. Before they got there, Max heard a loud cry as Abby came flying out of the masses, diving on one of the approaching soldiers. He screamed as she downed the one man, the others stopping in shock at seeing an uninfected attacking one of their own. The moment of distraction was enough, and Cam and Tara quickly came forward and dispatched the others just as Max and Bear arrived.

Standing up and pushing a stray hair out of her face, Abby turned to Max.

"We can't keep this up," she told him, her chest heaving. He could see she was splattered with gore, as they all were. Both sides had sustained heavy losses and the moans of those injured were notable even over the clash of the ongoing battle.

Max turned to see where the rest of their people were, just in time to see Bear stepping up behind Cords, who was furiously shouting orders and not paying attention to the man coming up at his back.

With unprecedented grace, Bear wrapped his arms around the man, holding a sinister looking blade to his neck. Without needing to say anything, the troops around them stepped back. Luckily for Cords, he was well respected and liked among his people and the new arrivals followed their lead. The infected around them stepped back towards Max on his loud command, and once again the sides stood off but this time, Cords was on their side of the standoff.

"Don't do anything stupid and I won't have to hurt your Captain," Bear growled out at the soldiers circling them. Max watched with unease, unsure of what to do or how to make the fighting stop.

"Stand back," Cords yelled to the soldiers who were watching intently. "I am your Captain, stand back I say!"

Max felt someone step up behind him, glancing long enough to see Michele, who was still holding her arm to her chest. She looked pale and unwell, though whether that was from the infection or the blood loss, he wasn't sure.

"Cords!" she yelled, her voice hoarse. Many turned their heads towards the noise, everyone waiting to see what would happen next.

"You never liked me, I know. But you always respected my opinion and knowledge." She paused for effect, looking up at Max. "These people don't need to fight. They just wanted their children back." She gestured behind her to where Tara and Cam stood in front of the two infected children.

All those who looked only saw two uninfected people, risking their lives to save what they considered zombie children. Cords stilled his struggles and looked at the unlikely image. Max saw a flash of something in his eyes as he took in the sight of the two young girls, and his body seemed to deflate.

"Let us leave," Michele finished, the pleading tone evident in her voice.

Around them, shouts of outrage came from the soldiers. Cords held up a hand to silence them. Max's respect increased for the man at seeing how he commanded his men, even with a knife to his throat.

"Bear, let him go, but keep him close. Captain, what do you say you and I have a talk?" Cords stepped away from Bear with what dignity he could muster before nodding at Max.

"Weapons down until I say otherwise, or unless you are directly attacked," Cords said to the men, never taking his eyes off Max.

Chapter 34

Clara, Tonya, Seventeen, and Sam stood at the top of the slope, clinging to one another as they watched the scene unfold below them. For several minutes, Clara lost sight of Max, and Seventeen had to hold her back from rushing down to find him. She felt so useless sitting there waiting, but when Seventeen pointed out she would only be in the way she stayed put. When she saw Bear help her husband up, who seemed mostly unharmed, she finally breathed a sigh of relief.

The sounds of the battle diminished as both sides took a breath, facing one another. She could see Bear held a man in his grasp, someone she didn't recognize. A blonde woman, who seemed vaguely familiar, stepped forward and spoke but Clara couldn't hear what was said. She did hear the angry cries of the uninfected at her words though, and squeezed Tonya's hand tighter. Clara was sure the other woman's focus was solely on the other small girl below, whom she assumed to be Halee.

She watched as Bear released the man who strode over to Max. For several moments the four men spoke, and the entire valley waited on pins and needles to see what would happen next.

It seemed like hours passed, but really it was mere minutes before she watched in shock as her husband held out his hand for the uninfected man before him. The man barked orders at his men and Max shouted something and she watched as he began to lead the infected out the open gates.

Not willing to wait a moment longer, she let go of Seventeen's hand and started running down the hill towards her family.

* * *

Max stood at the gate with Bear letting the others pass through, doing what he could to get them moving as quickly as possible. Their current truce was not something Max wanted to count on, not with the hoard of angry uninfected still glaring at them from the compound doors. Most obviously did not agree with their leader, and Max didn't know how long the order to stand down would last.

Tara and her soldier approached, Joan in the latter's arms. Max gave the man a nod of appreciation before taking his daughter. Tara held Halee's hand and the three passed through with the crowd of infected with them. Abby stopped in front of them.

"What happened?" she asked curiously. Max only shook his head. "Later. For now, we have a truce. How long that will last, I don't know, but right now we need to get everyone out of here." Abby gave him a curt nod before working her way to the back of the group, herding the slower and still serum affected infected forward as quickly as she could. He noted Kenny was doing something similar and took a moment to look down at his daughter in his arms. Max did his best to fight the tears building behind his eyes at his gratefulness when something fast slammed into them both.

A familiar smell filled his nostrils followed by his wife's sobs. Adjusting Joan in his arm, he brought his other around Clara and held her tightly to his chest too.

Clara sniffed and looked up into his face, seemingly not ashamed of the tears flowing down her own face.

"You did it," she whispered as she brought her hand up and stroked his cheek, heedless of the blood and gore covering him. Max gave her a small smile.

"Of course I did," he told her, kissing her forehead. "I keep my promises."

Max turned taking one last look around and noted Cords was still watching him with a strange look on his face. For a moment, Max felt oddly protective of the small moment the man had just seen him share with his family, but the captain only nodded. Max returned it and turned to take up the head of the group.

It was time to go home.

$* * *$

Joan groaned lightly as she woke, making sure to keep her eyes tightly shut as she had learned how vicious the brightness of artificial light was. As her mind became clearer, she noticed a freshness to the air that she hadn't smelled in a long time, and a quick and short bird song shot her into full wakefulness. Sitting up, she opened her eyes, rubbing them in disbelief, to see her father kneeling in front of her, her mother beside him.

A sob immediately fell from her throat and weeks of fear unleashed as she threw herself into her parents' arms. Her mother's voice gently hushed her as she stroked her head. She looked up to see the tears falling from her father's eyes. For a moment, this shocked Joan; she had never seen her father cry before. He had always been so strong and sure. Reaching her arm over she wiped a tear from his face, eliciting a small laugh and smile from him. He used the back of his hand to wipe his face before bringing his hand up and stroking her cheek.

"We missed you, little bug," her father said, his voice threatening to crack. Joan buried herself deeper into her mother's arms and closed her eyes.

She was safe now.

Chapter 35

Less than two weeks before, twelve people had left the Squamish infected community. Today, Max led a group of almost seventy people back. Not one of their original numbers had been lost, only a few injuries, and a lot of people missed were regained. Despite the serum-fed infected, the group made good time going back, and in under three days they were being welcomed back into the community.

Seventeen, Aaron and Kenny ended up taking on much of the infected group for the homeward journey. With no serum being fed to them, and the combination of fresh air and food, many regained their senses quickly, and while it was apparent many were slower to begin with, they were all pleased that there seemed no long-lasting effects from the serum.

The community was prepared for their arrival. The scouts had obviously told them there was a larger group coming and by the time they got to the front gate, there were a dozen people waiting for them, ready to greet the new arrivals.

* * *

Everyone settled in quickly. With the influx of new arrivals, large tents and temporary structures had been set up outside the community walls until proper accommodations could be made. At least thirty of the infected they had brought back with them had been from the community originally, leaving another thirty or so people who were slowly but surely integrating themselves within the community.

Clara helped where she could but had to force herself to be more than a few feet away from Joan. Sitting outside their small assigned cabin, Clara watched as Joan, Halee, and Cassie ran around the open field behind the row of homes. Despite their different ages, the three girls quickly found things in common and were currently engrossed in a game of running back and forth. Clara's heart swelled at the sight of Joan getting along so well with others, finally getting to experience a bit of the joys of playing with other children. Looking over to confirm Ike was still nearby watching, Clara waved to indicate she would be back. He waved back and nodded at her; he would watch them. It was time to talk to Max.

It didn't take long for her to find Max, who was sitting outside of the medical tent. Clara already knew Michele was inside and was due to pass at any time. Clara was saddened that she may not get a chance to get to know the woman further. On their journey home she found out that Michele was Rachel's sister, and she had looked forward to getting to know her. As it was with all those who contracted the virus, whether she would rise again minutes later was unknown. Clara didn't yet know exactly what part the woman had played in keeping her daughter captive, but knowing she was Rachel's sister said a lot. If Max was willing to trust her then so would she.

"Any news?" Clara asked as she approached, taking the seat next to him. Max shook his head, immediately putting his hand into Clara's. She had noticed he was often touching her and Joan in small affectionate ways since they had gotten back, as though constantly reassuring himself they were there. Not that she minded, and in fact had plans to get him alone for a lot more touching later that evening.

"No, nothing yet, but it'll be today." Clara gave his hand a gentle squeeze. "Nothing we can do but wait and see."

The couple sat in silence for several moments, each lost in their own thoughts. Clara was considering how to approach the subject she had come over for, but Max beat her to it.

"Nice to see Joan playing with kids finally," he said casually, looking out at the far field where the small figures played. Clara smiled. "Yes, I'm glad she gets to be a real kid, for at least a little while." Max turned to her, a funny sort of expression on his face as Clara eyed him suspiciously before sighing.

"You know, don't you?"

At this, Max smirked at her. "Why don't you ask what you came over to ask, dear?" Clara did her best not to bristle at the condescending tone to the question. Max knew her better than she knew herself at times. It shouldn't surprise her that her line of thought was obvious to him.

"I want to stay," she told him, looking into his face for any signs of a reaction. His smirk fell, falling into a more resigned smile.

"I know." Max replied simply without responding to her statement. Clara prodded him with her elbow, causing Max to let out a small laugh.

"I know you do, baby," he repeated. "I've known since we got here you would want to stay."

"And?"

Lifting their clasped hands, Max kissed her knuckles. "And you should know by now that for you, for Joan, I would do anything. I'm sorry for how I've acted the last few years. You were right, we need to be around other people and I need to learn to let go. I love you, Clara." Clara's grin in response seemed to please him and he quickly enveloped her in a huge hug.

"I love you so much," she whispered into his neck, fighting the tears that threatened to spill over. She knew he would never stop worrying about her and Joan and she would never expect him to. Hearing those words from him though felt like a weight lifted from her heart that she had carried so long. She felt like a lucky woman to have a man that cared for her so deeply, yet wasn't afraid to admit he was wrong.

"Max, come quick," a voice said from inside the medical tent beside them. Clara stepped away and watched as Max's face fell into a hard expression.

"Go find Joan and give her the good news. I'll find you when I'm done here," Max told her as he stood. Giving him a quick nod and one final reassuring squeeze, Clara went off to find Joan.

* * *

Max walked into the tent, blinking his eyes a few times to get used to the dimmer lighting inside. It didn't take long for his eyes to adjust as he made his way over to Michele's bedside. Simple cots had been made of wood, and though they had seemed small to him when he first saw them, it amazed him how tiny Michele looked inside of hers. Her skin was pale and a sheen of sweat covered her brow, but still she gave him a small smile as he approached.

Max's heart cracked as he remembered seeing Jay just like this, so many years before. He made a mental note to himself to remake Jay's gravestone in the community graveyard. No matter how many years had passed, he would never stop being grateful to Jay and all the boy had done for him. Shaking his head, he strode up to the bed, all of his focus now on the woman in front of him.

"Looks like this is it," Michele rasped as Max leaned over to take her hand.

"Just the beginning of a new chapter," Max told her confidently. Michele tried to smile but instead got carried away in a coughing fit. Terry, the resident doctor, sat in the corner waiting, but said nothing. Max recalled Clara once telling him that all doctors knew that there was a point where there simply wasn't anything else they could do for their patient but be present. He was no doctor, but being here with her was the least he could do after she helped them.

Max sat with her, rubbing his thumb over her frail hand and helping her sit up when she needed to cough or throw up. Though Michele said nothing else, he felt her gratitude at not being alone in this.

An hour later, she died.

Chapter 36

Everything began to settle into a more normal routine after the events at the compound. Once back from the base, it seemed everyone in the community came to Max for advice, to thank him or congratulate on their success. Every time it was the latter, he very firmly explained how it was a group effort and that Clara and himself were merely the ones to get the ball rolling. This didn't seem to matter to anyone, though.

Max and Clara had brought with them inspiration and a vision for a better future for their people. Since Guy had started getting ill earlier in the year, morale had been low and their missing people only made things worse.

In a more formal setting, Max explained all that had happened when he spoke to Captain Cords, the leader of the uninfected compound. Both sides recognized that if they continued fighting, there would be no one left on either side. Cords had agreed to let them leave, but made it clear that any infected that stepped foot within their valley after that day was at their own risk. Cords made no promises for the future or for the rest of the infected, only that for this day, they could leave. Max sensed there was more to the man's words than this, but kept that to himself.

Max respected Cords and believed he made no promises he couldn't keep, and they shook their agreement in the first formal truce between the infected and uninfected. It was only a temporary truce, but for now the immediate threat was gone. The future of both sides was uncertain, and Max knew this was far from the last trouble they would have with uninfected.

One week after they got back, Guy passed quietly in his sleep. While the community was heartbroken at the loss of the man who had brought many of them together, they all knew it was coming. Rather than mourn him, they held a celebration of life to honor him and all he had done to bring their people together.

Max sat at the edge of the gathering and only watched, letting it all roll over him. Leaving their home, almost losing Joan, new friends made like Bear and Kenny, the first truce with the uninfected…All of what had happened in the past six weeks poured over his mind, unable to settle.

Joan saw her father sitting on the edge of the gathering and approached him with soft steps.

"Daddy?" she asked hesitantly, making him look up. Max smiled at his daughter and patted the seat beside him. Joan quickly grinned and hopped over, happy to have her father's arms around her.

"Why are you sad, daddy?" she asked after a moment. Max considered this for a moment before kissing her head.

"I'm not sad, baby. Just thinking," he answered honestly.

"What are you thinking about?"

Max couldn't help but smile. "I'm just happy that we're all here and all safe."

"Oh. Me too," Joan replied. They sat in amicable silence for several minutes until Max cleared his throat, turning his face towards Joan's.

"I'm sorry I treated you like a baby," Max said, and Joan's eyes widened, "you will always be my baby, but I should have trusted you to be old enough to know everything. I'm sorry I kept so much from you. This all never would have happened if I'd told you more about the uninfected in the first place."

Tears swam in Joan's eyes as she listened to her father's words. "It's not your fault daddy," she said, leaning further into his arms, "and you can call me baby if you want to."

Max smiled and kissed her forehead, chuckling as she nuzzled further into his chest, falling asleep only moments later. With his arms wrapped around his daughter, Max watched the flames feeling a contentment he hadn't felt in a long time. He was terrified for the future, but somehow that seemed okay. He looked over towards the small community cemetery and said his final goodbyes to Guy and his life as he had known it the last seven years.

* * *

The morning after, a vote was held to replace Guy's position with four people among their community who would act as a sort of senate rather than one person taking up the mantle. The moment Lake realized he wouldn't be one of them, he immediately left the gathering. Clara had told Max a bit about the man and he would be surprised if Lake was still in the community at all by the end of the week.

Max was quickly voted in, and despite his hesitations, Clara spoke to him, softly encouraging him to do it. He was a natural leader, she told him, and he had people's best interests at heart. Reluctantly, he agreed.

Sam declined the position, saying she had enough on her plate as it was, and instead nominated Angela. A fierce woman and mother, she was among the first in the community. Angela was well respected and graciously accepted.

Abby was nominated by Seventeen, who felt that one of the uninfected in the community should be represented in the group. Though she was flustered by it, Abby also accepted with happy tears in her eyes. She later hugged Seventeen and admitted that the feeling of acceptance was one she had been waiting her whole life for.

The last position was filled by Aaron, whose background and skills made him a great candidate. He was strong and fierce, and also agreed to take over the security of the community.

Max, Angela, Abby, and Aaron joined hands with smiles on their faces and the joyous cries of their people in their ears.

In honour of their new hierarchy and expanding community, a decision was made to formally name themselves, and everyone was in the process of coming up with names and voting. Max and the other leaders were happy to leave that to the people.

It was the beginning of a new phase post-FIRE for the uninfected on the lower mainland of British Columbia, and though there were still many problems to worry about, the uneasy truce with the uninfected community only being one of many, the future was bright.

Chapter 37

"So, when it's inside the brackets, you calculate that first before doing the rest," Michele was explaining to Joan as Max walked by the gathering. He smiled at them but said nothing as he passed, not wanting to interrupt their lesson. Bear was working on expanding Sam's teaching area, but in the meantime, Michele agreed to work with Joan on math and some other things that he and Clara had been unable to teach her in their remote wilderness home.

Michele had died for several minutes before rising again, much to Max's relief. She had been one of the lucky ones, regaining her function and most of her memories relatively quickly. Whether it was her intelligence pre-FIRE, or the short time she remained dead, they didn't know, but everyone was happy to welcome a talented scientist into their community. Despite her history at the compound, she was welcomed. After all, they had all done things they regretted in the world of FIRE.

When Joan saw Bear again she was wary at first, but even told her parents he was nice to her. Much to Max's surprise, Joan and the big man became fast friends and Bear was already teaching her more about hunting. Max would catch Bear watching Joan with sorrow in his eyes and knew he was mourning his own lost child.

As Max walked toward the gate, he greeted or nodded at many as he passed. It was so strange to him to think that barely over a month ago, it was just him, Clara, and Joan; now, their family had grown exponentially. Though he knew that more people also meant more problems, not to mention risks, it was worth it to see the smiles on his beautiful daughter and wife's faces. On his people's faces.

As he was thinking this, he finally got to his destination to see Clara grinning broadly as she oversaw the last of the herb planting. The sparkle in her eye from a good day's work was evident and made his heart swell.

After some initial butting of heads, Terry had reluctantly agreed to make her a regular part of the medical team. Clara did her best not to patronize the man, grateful just to have a place where she could be useful, and gladly took the job of organizing the planting and preparation for herbal medicines that would benefit all. She was delighted when she found out Cam also had a similar background, and the two of them spent hours discussing what they would need to start to build a real pharmacy. Sam had been a bit distracted with her own life lately, and Clara was happy to have someone to talk to about her passion. The freedom in growing things and creating helped Clara truly blossom.

"Hey baby! Look, we finally finished!" Clara held out her arms in presentation of her garden as Max stepped up, wrapping his arm around her shoulders and kissing her forehead.

"That's great," he said, smiling. "I just wanted to know if you wanted to join Sam and them for dinner tonight? She's having a little gathering with a few people and asked if we wanted to come. I said I'd check with you first."

"We'll be there too," Cam said as he stood up, wiping the sweat from his brow. "Tara is even making some kind of blackberry dessert."

"Well now we definitely have to go," Max said with a grin and a wink. "I've heard your girl has a way with food." Cam flushed slightly but smiled, grateful for the inclusion he had felt since coming here.

"It's true," Cam replied, patting his belly, "she's going to make me fat soon if I'm not careful."

Clara smiled, kissing Max lightly on the cheek. "Let me go get cleaned up and I'll meet you over there."

That night there were almost twenty people at Sam's dinner. Max noted Sam seemed a bit flustered, but when he offered to help, she politely declined. Bear had spent the better part of two days hunting, finally trapping a fat beaver that Sam slow roasted to perfection. Everyone contributed other food items and by the end of the meal, groans were audible. Max sat holding

Joan, who had promptly fallen asleep in his arms after eating.

Around the table people chatted comfortably until Sam stood and took a place at the front of the table, Bear standing just slightly behind her. Max noted the man fidgeting with his shirt and a knowing smile came to his face as he realized what the occasion was

"Thank you all for coming tonight," she began. "We are so grateful for the opportunity to spend an evening with our family, all of you, but there is actually another reason we asked you all here tonight." Smiling, she turned to Bear and held out her hand to him which he immediately grasped, bringing her knuckle to his lips. Turning to the group, Bear's face split into a huge grin.

"She said yes!"

* * *

Max and Clara whispered to one another late into the night. While Clara hadn't gotten as much alone time with Max as she would have liked this week, it was worth it to have their family together. Since Joan fell asleep earlier, Max had deposited her into her own little bed as opposed to theirs like he had been recently.

"Do you think it will last?" Clara whispered, her legs intertwined with Max's as he lightly rubbed her thigh.

"What's that?" Max asked distractedly, always and forever entranced by his wife's soft skin. Giggling, she pushed his hand away, making him grin devilishly.

"The truce, peace, all of it," she asked. Max paused from his ministrations for a moment and looked into Clara face. Smiling, he lifted his hand to her chin and brought her face to his. Pulling away, he made a small sigh.

"No," he finally replied honestly, "but for now, it's enough."

Prologue

"You're sure the test was hers?" the doctor, Harold Green, asked Cords skeptically. With a tense jaw he nodded.

"I'm sure," Cords snapped. "Now, can you tell me how a zombie was able to get pregnant?"

Green flipped through the papers one more time before looking up at him. "Without more data, more specimens, I can't be positive. But it's my guess that where we previously thought it wasn't possible for the infected to procreate, it seems more likely that infected males are not able to. In theory, an infected woman could be impregnated by an uninfected man." Green's face twisted in disgust as he said the words and it took everything in Cords not to react. "We simply haven't seen such depravity here. I mean, who in their right minds would ever have sex with..." before Green could finish, Cords reached over and snapped his neck. The man's body dropped, and Cords sighed before walking around his desk to take a seat.

It had been almost a week since the infected had broken out, or been let out as some had accused Cords, and he had barely a moment's peace since. Between digging graves, cleaning up the base, and bringing in the new soldiers, he had his work cut out for him, and had no time to think about Nikki, or what he had found out.

Cords pulled out the last few drops of whiskey from his desk and poured them as he picked up the papers dropped by the former Doctor Green.

What this meant for the future, Cords didn't know.

Taking a swig of the hearty drink, he pulled out a match and set fire to the papers, watching all evidence of Nikki's pregnancy go up in smoke.

The world isn't ready, he thought, *but tomorrow, or the next day? Who knows?*

And the sun sets again on the world of Dead Aware! Thank you SO much for reading and please do leave a review! It helps us indie authors more than you could ever know.

I hope you enjoyed the continuation of Max and Clara's journey, as well as all of the new (and resurfaced) characters. I absolutely love writing in the Dead Aware world and have plans for many more future stories! Max and Clara (and Joan) will likely have one more book, maybe two. I also have a few side stories I am working on within the same world including a prequel for Bear and for Jay, as well as some totally new characters. I also want to write an origin story for how FIRE came to be, as all we ever really found out was that it originated in India.

Is there a Dead Aware story you want to see? Tell me about it!

You can contact me at elemerry@gmail.com or find me on social media

I want to give a huge thanks to the people who have supported me on this journey. My family and friends and especially my amazing fans. Your kind words and encouragement are what keep me going!

Huge thanks to Cassie Angler, who has helped me maintain my sanity throughout all of the projects I've been juggling. Your love and support means more than I can say.

My beta readers; Jaye, Aaron, Melissa - You guys are the freakin' best!

Special thanks to my mom, Tina, who is not only an amazing beta reader for me but is always there for me to bounce random idea's and edits off of. I love you mom!

Also a huge thanks to everyone who let me use their names in this one! Stephen Cords, Nikki Noir, Aaron Bader, Kenny Hughes. Sam Madrus (and Max Madrus, who is actually Bear in this story!), Halee Heising, Tonya Sanger, Brian and Sarah Scutt and Michele Foster. You all rock and I hope you like your fictional counterparts!

Big shout out to my cover artist, Brian Scutt. You've spoiled me on all artistic collaborations for life, you're stuck with me now. Thanks for dealing with all my revisions and random orders. You are truly the best.

To my editor, Alexander Shedd. You do such an amazing job in keeping my voice on the pages while providing such constructive feedback and ideas. I am very grateful for all you do!

And to all my indie authors friends, there are too many of you to name but you know who you are.

You can follow me or check out my other books at the links below!

Until next time!

xxx

Eleanor Merry
AKA. Zombie Ele

Also by Eleanor Merry

Dead Aware:
   Dead Aware: A Zombie Journey
   Dead Aware: Zombie Mom (Free!)
   Dead Aware: Vagrant Youth

Holiday Horror Collection:
   Dark Valentine
   Dark X-Mas

Follow me:
Facebook
Instagram
Goodreads
Bookbub